NINA

IN That Makes Me Mad!

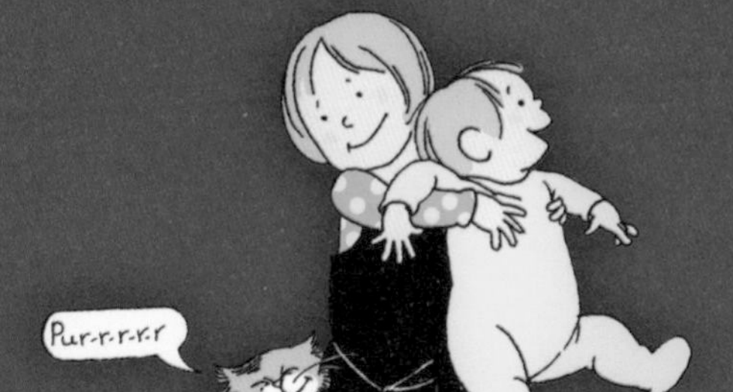

Pur-r-r-r-r

HILARY KNIGHT

STEVEN KROLL

NINA

IN

That Make

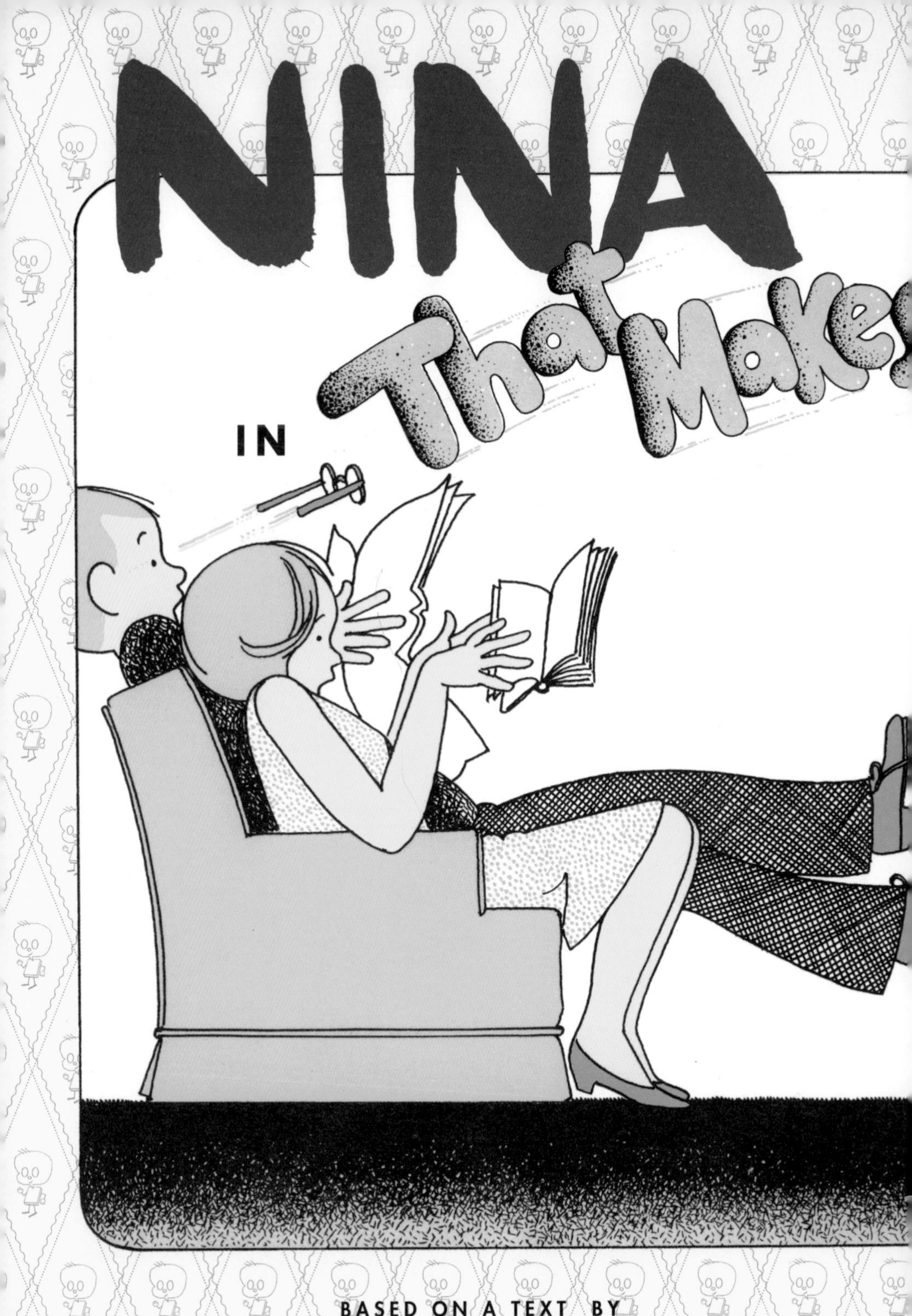

BASED ON A TEXT BY

STEVEN KROLL

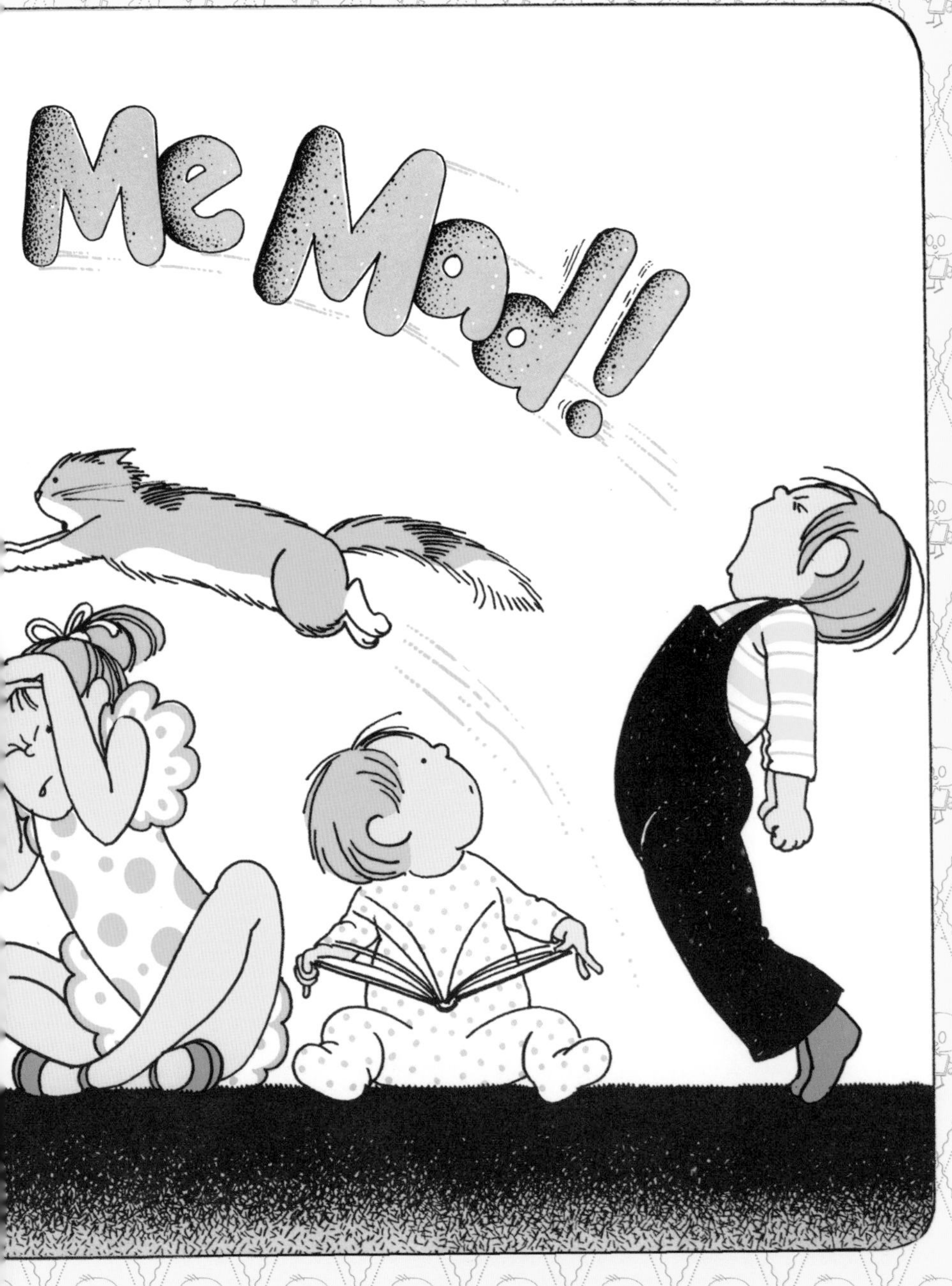
Me Mad!!

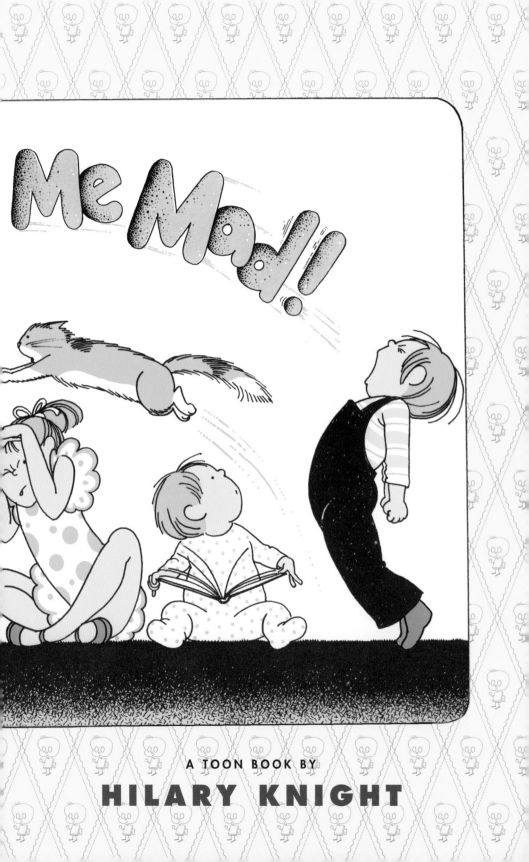

A TOON BOOK BY

HILARY KNIGHT

For my father, Clayton Knight
–Hilary Knight

For Kathleen. Forever.
–Steven Kroll

In memory of Steven Kroll (1941-2011),
a beloved and long-time member of
the children's book community.

Editorial Director: FRANÇOISE MOULY

Book Design: FRANÇOISE MOULY & LAURA FOXGROVER

 All our books are Smyth Sewn (the highest library-quality binding available) and printed with soy-based inks on acid-free woodfree paper harvested from responsible sources. Printed in China by C&C Offset Printing Co., Ltd. Distributed to the trade by Consortium Book Sales and Distribution, Inc.; orders (800) 283-3572; orderentry@perseusbooks.com; www.cbsd.com.

The Library of Congress has cataloged the hardcover edition as follows:
Knight, Hilary.
Nina in That makes me mad : a TOON book / by Hilary Knight ; based on a text by Steven Kroll.
p. cm.
Summary: Lots of little, everyday frustrations make Nina mad, and she is very good at expressing her feelings.
ISBN-13: 978-1-935179-10-8 (hardcover) ISBN-10: 1-935179-10-1 (hardcover)
1. Graphic novels. [1. Graphic novels. 2. Anger--Fiction. 3. Behavior--Fiction.] I. Kroll, Steven. II. Title. III. Title: That makes me mad.
PZ7.7.K66Ni 2011
741.5'973--dc22 2011000802

ISBN: 978-1-935179-10-8 (hardcover) ISBN: 978-1-943145-32-4 (paperback)

17 18 19 20 21 22 C&C 10 9 8 7 6 5 4 3 2 1

www.TOON-BOOKS.com

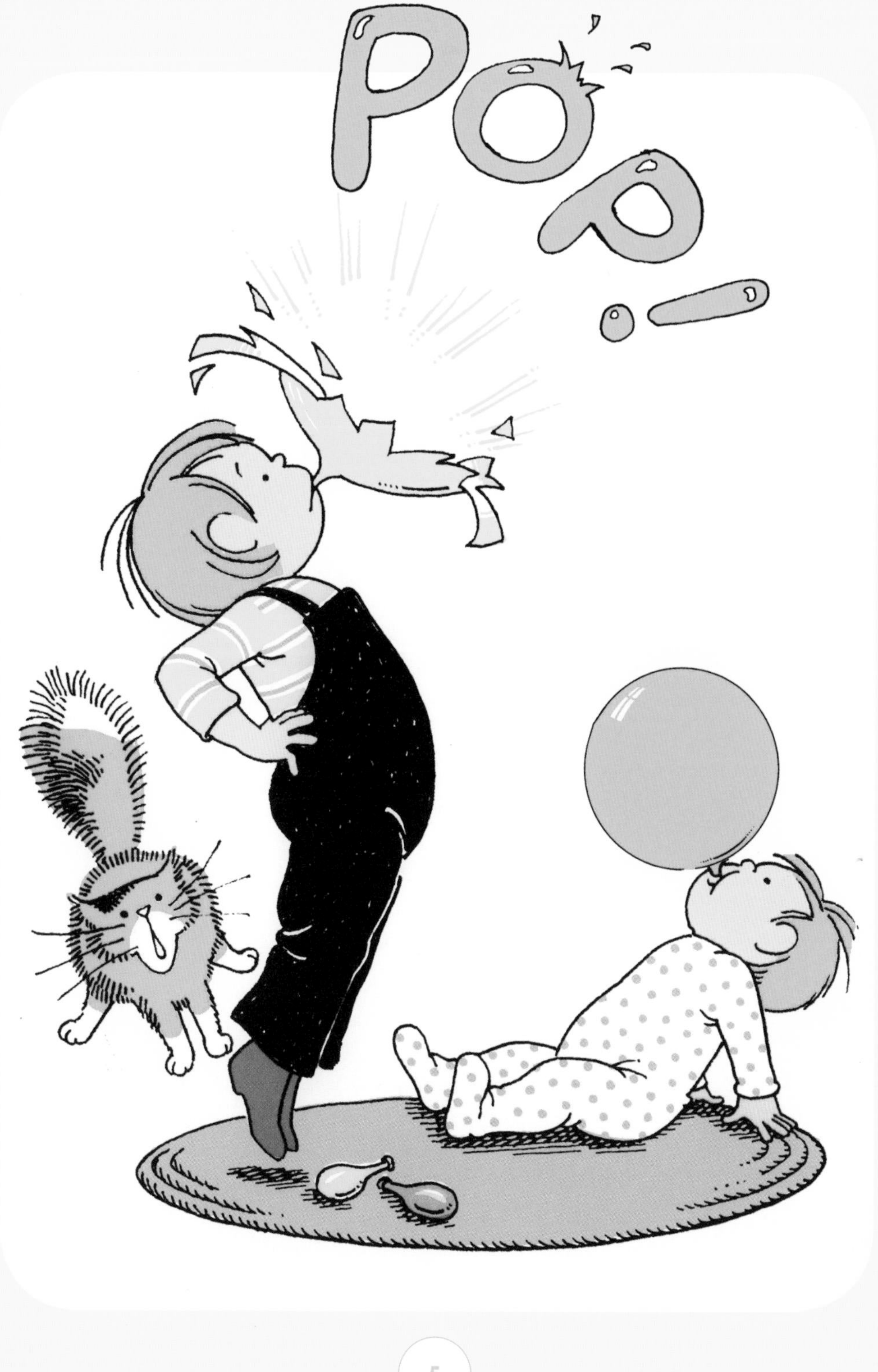
POP!

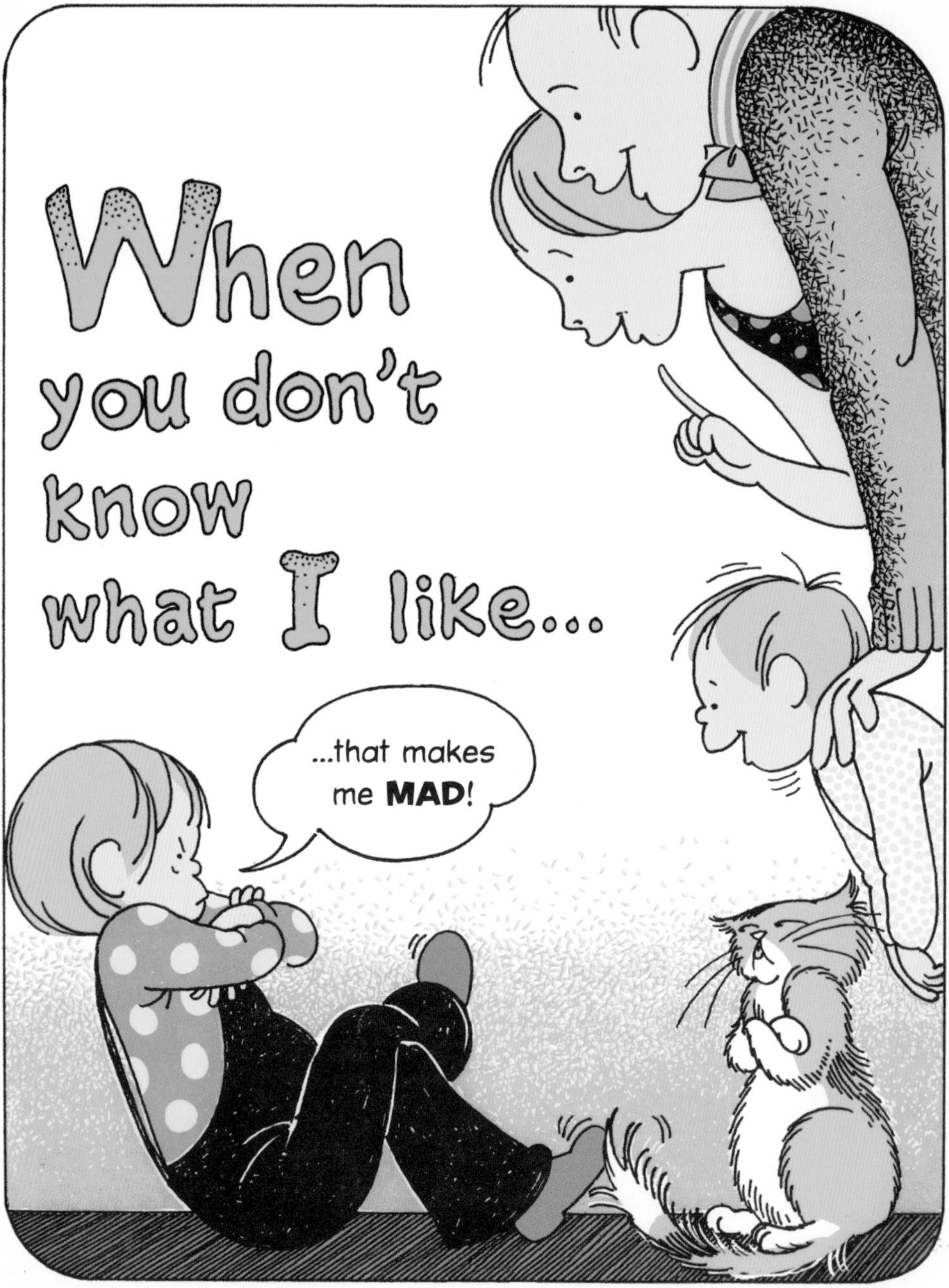
When you don't know what I like...
...that makes me MAD!

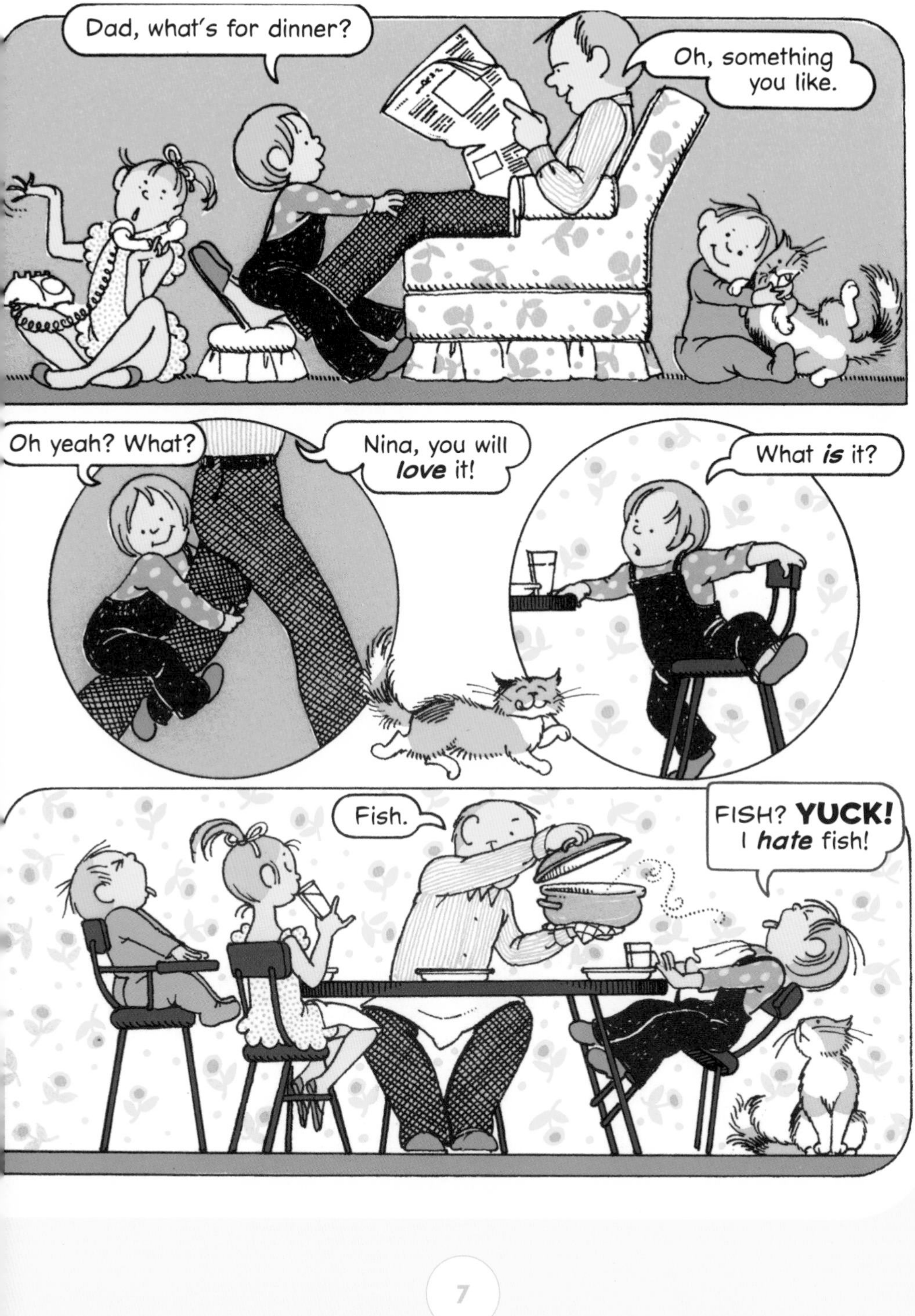
Dad, what's for dinner?
Oh, something you like.
Oh yeah? What?
Nina, you will *love* it!
What *is* it?
Fish.
FISH? **YUCK!** I *hate* fish!

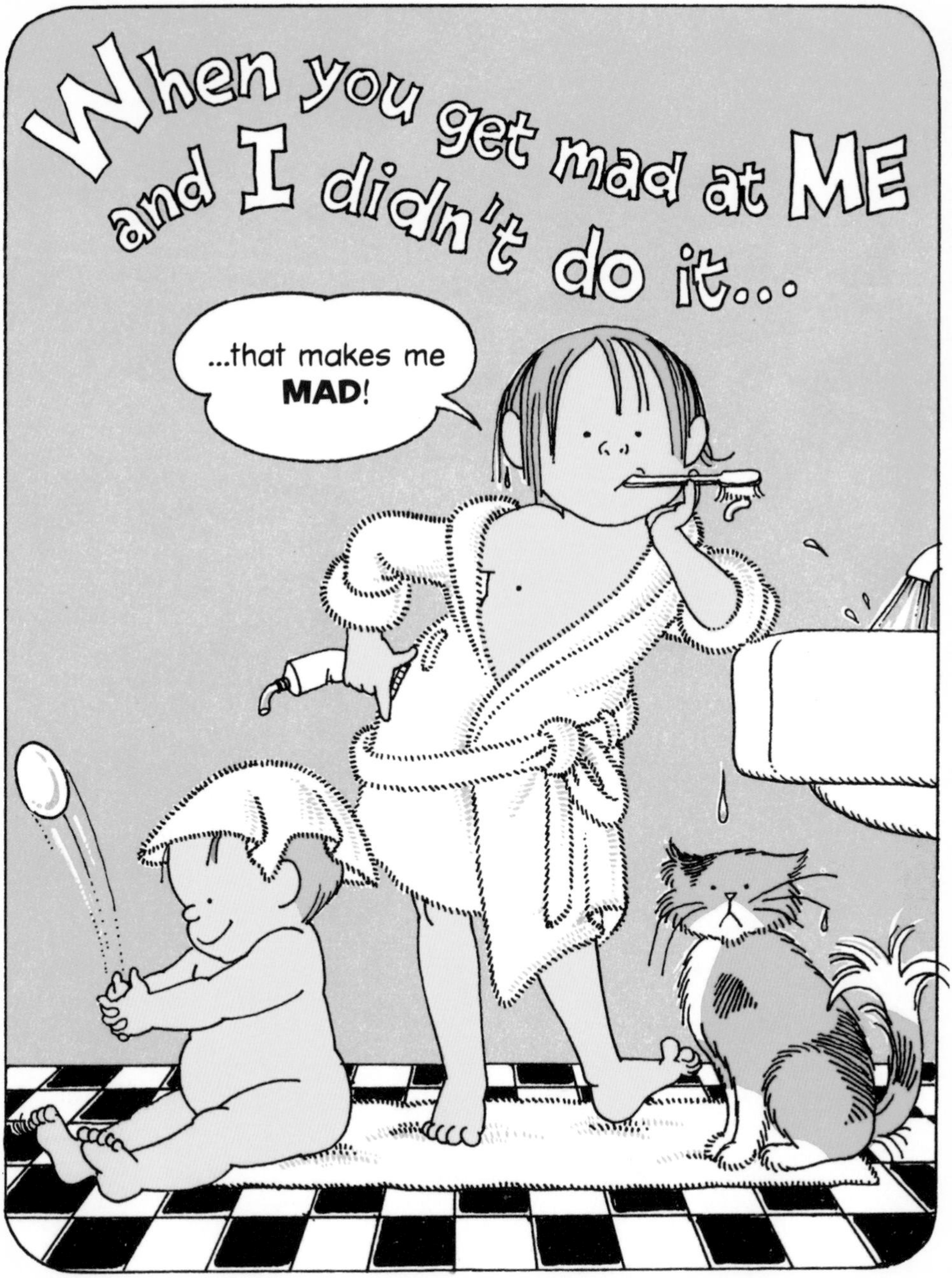
When you get mad at ME and I didn't do it...
...that makes me **MAD**!

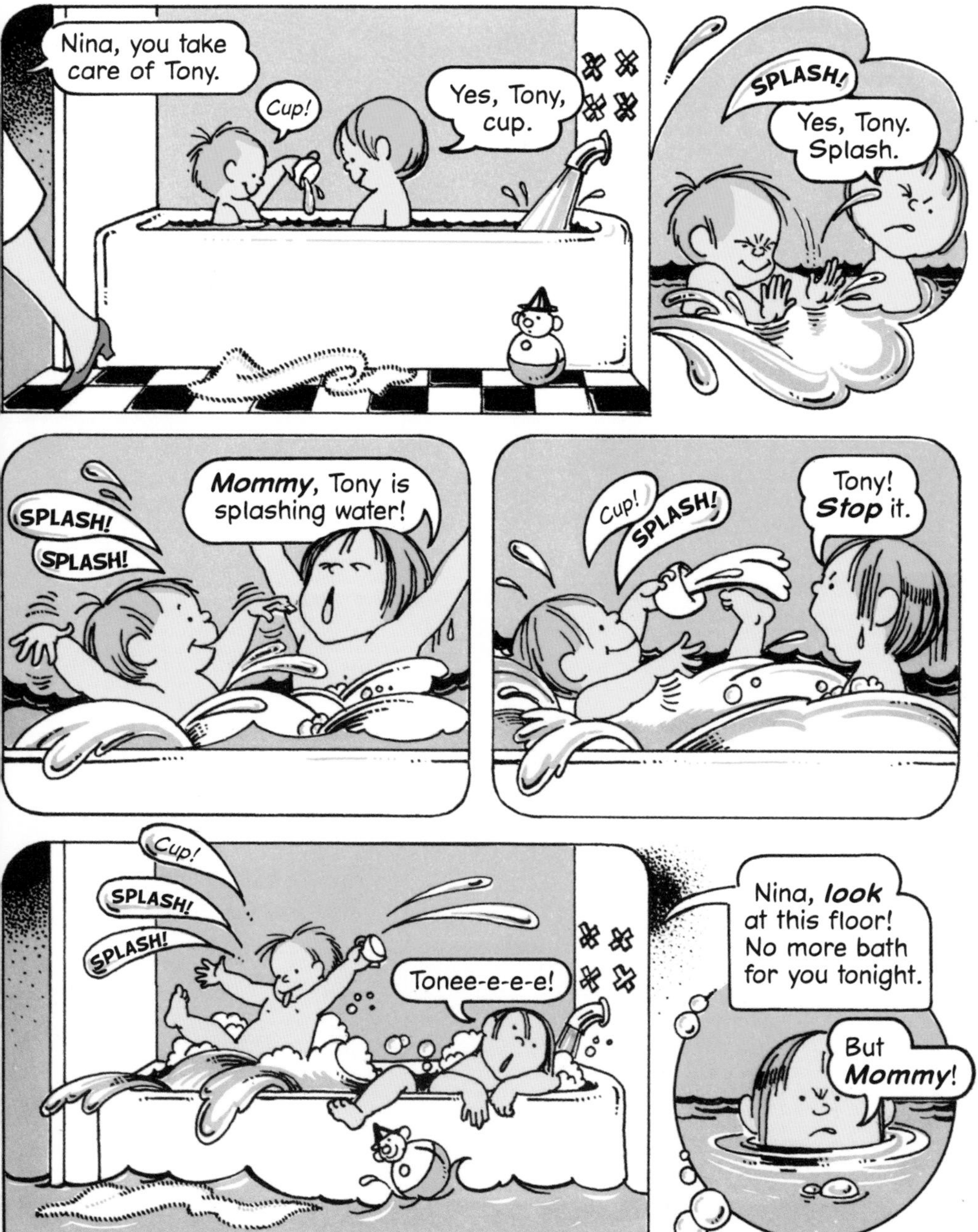
Nina, you take care of Tony.
Cup!
Yes, Tony, cup.
SPLASH!
Yes, Tony. Splash.
SPLASH!
SPLASH!
Mommy, Tony is splashing water!
Cup!
SPLASH!
Tony! Stop it.
Cup!
SPLASH!
SPLASH!
Tonee-e-e-e!
Nina, look at this floor! No more bath for you tonight.
But Mommy!

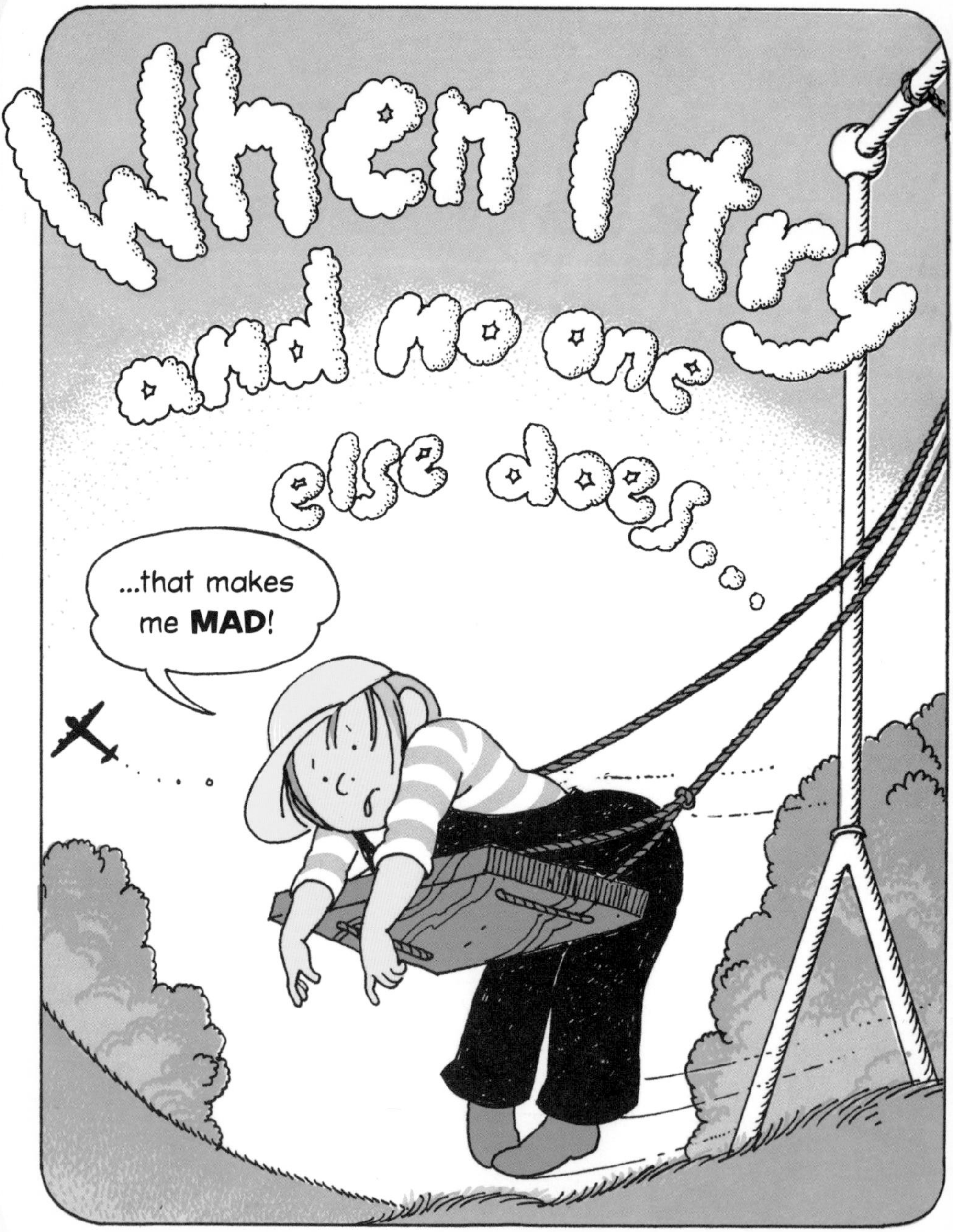
When I try and no one else does...
...that makes me **MAD**!

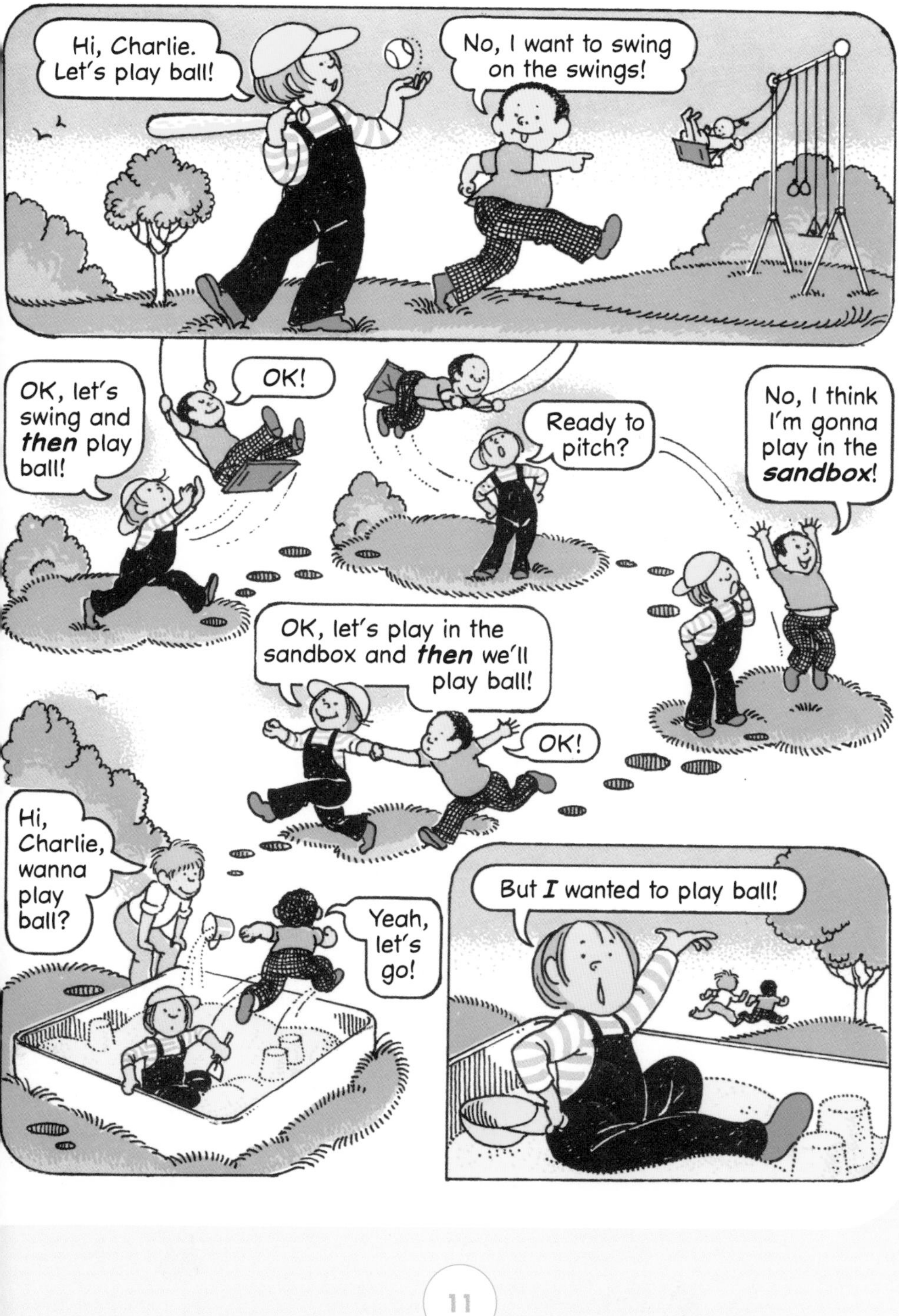
Hi, Charlie. Let's play ball!
No, I want to swing on the swings!
OK, let's swing and *then* play ball!
OK!
Ready to pitch?
No, I think I'm gonna play in the *sandbox*!
OK, let's play in the sandbox and *then* we'll play ball!
OK!
Hi, Charlie, wanna play ball?
Yeah, let's go!
But *I* wanted to play ball!

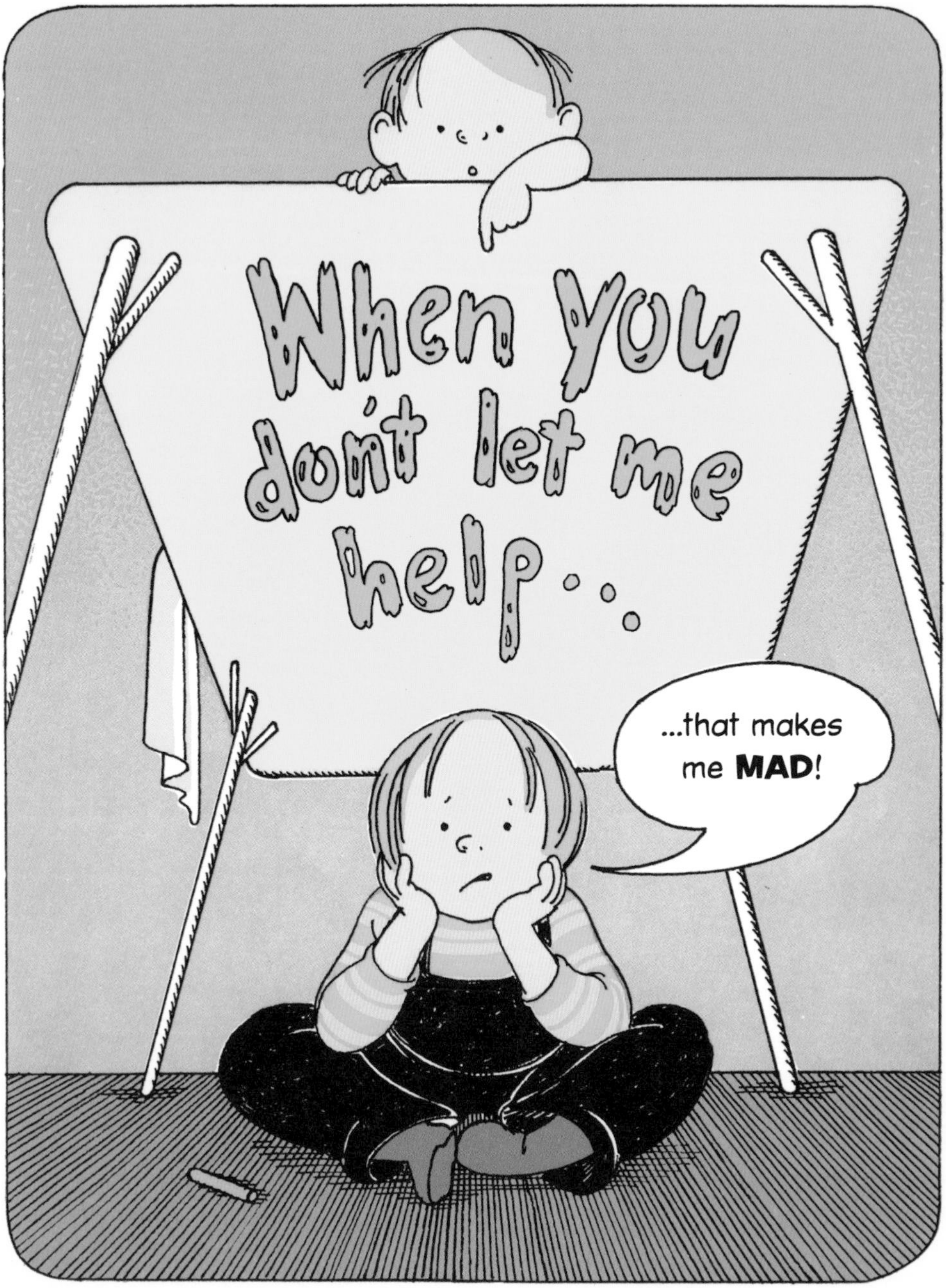
When you don't let me help...
...that makes me **MAD**!

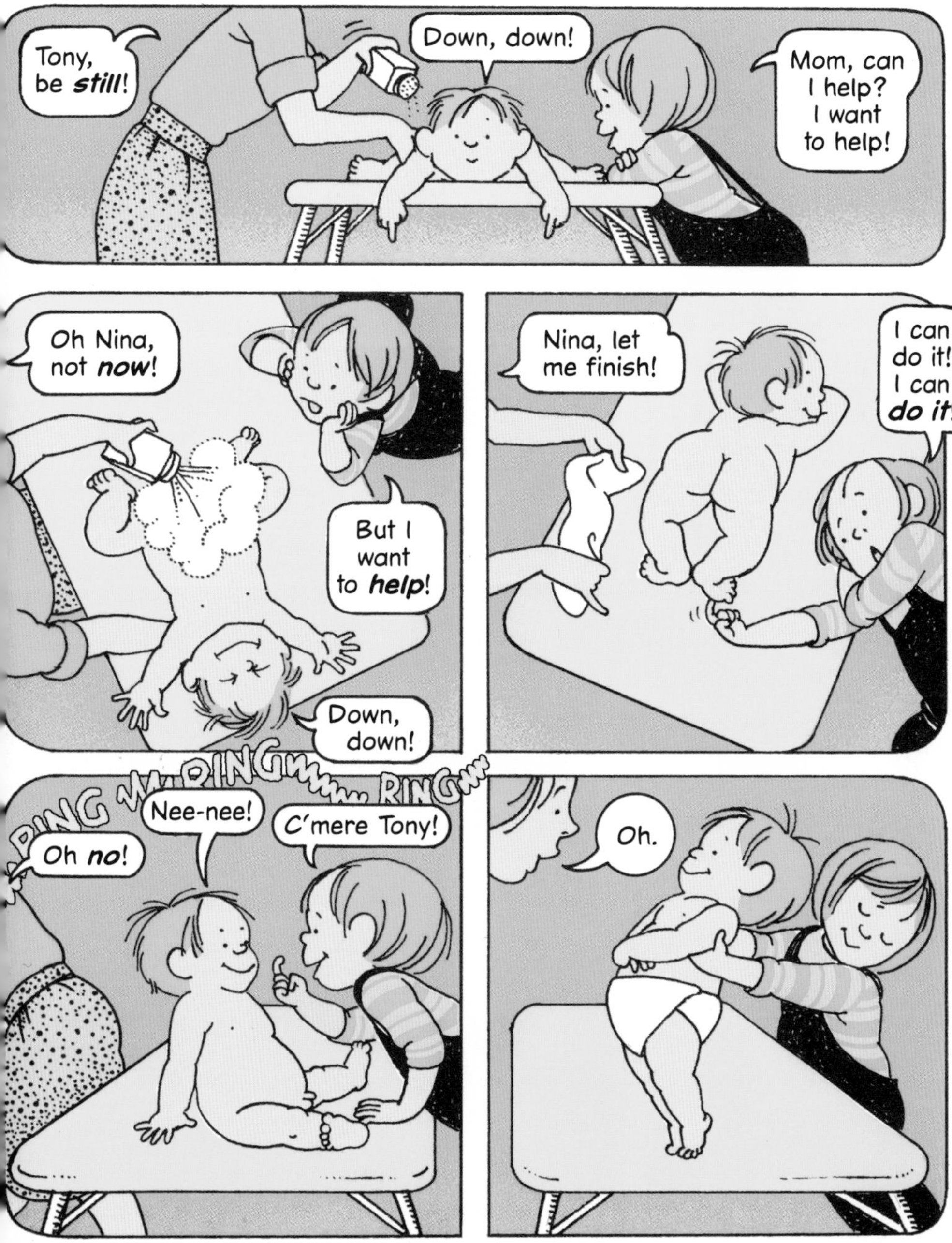
Tony,
be *still*!
Down, down!
Mom, can I help? I want to help!
Oh Nina, not *now*!
But I want to *help*!
Down, down!
Nina, let me finish!
I can do it! I can *do it*!
RING RING RING
Oh *no*!
Nee-nee!
C'mere Tony!
Oh.

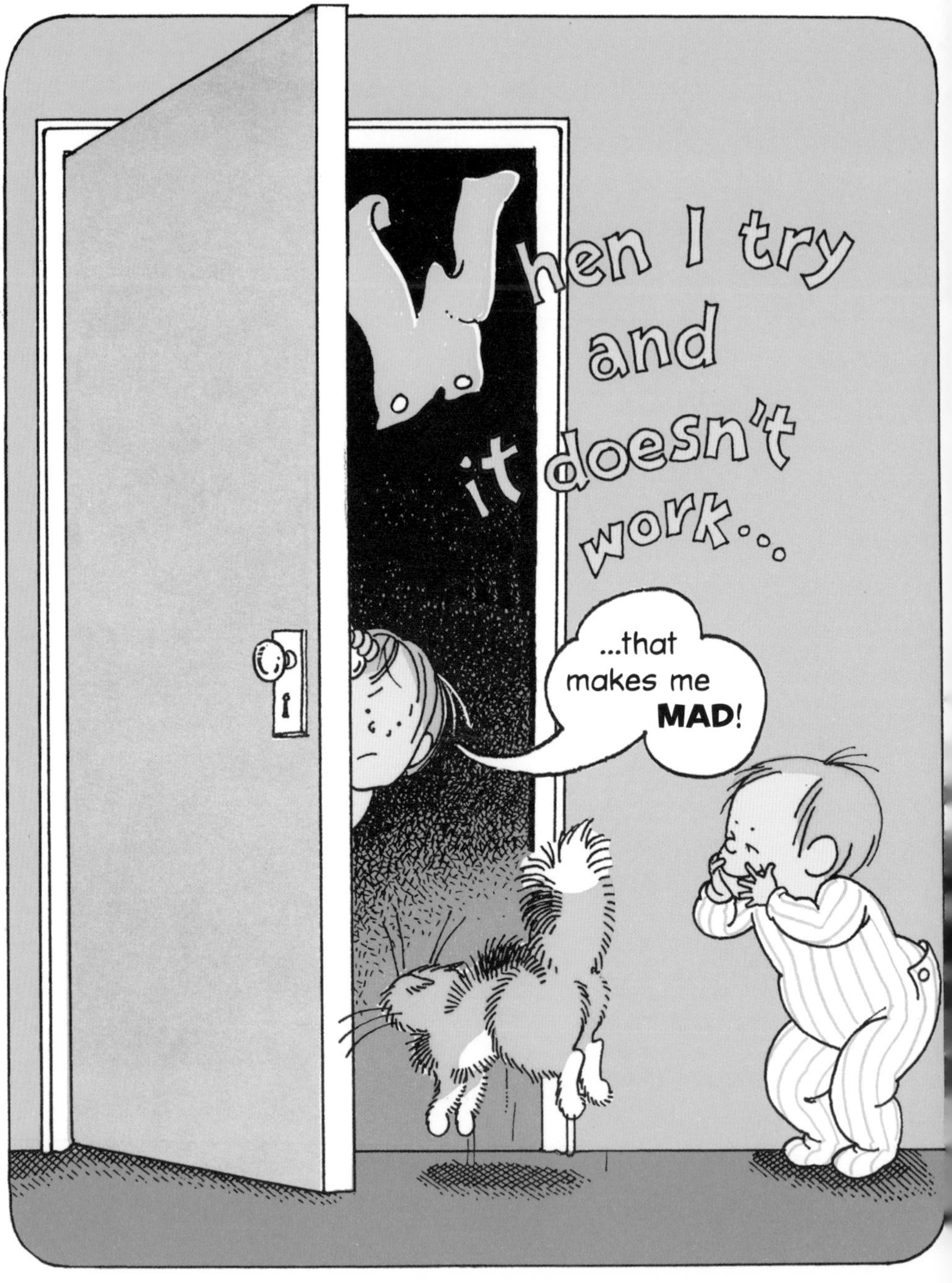
When I try and it doesn't work...
...that makes me **MAD**!

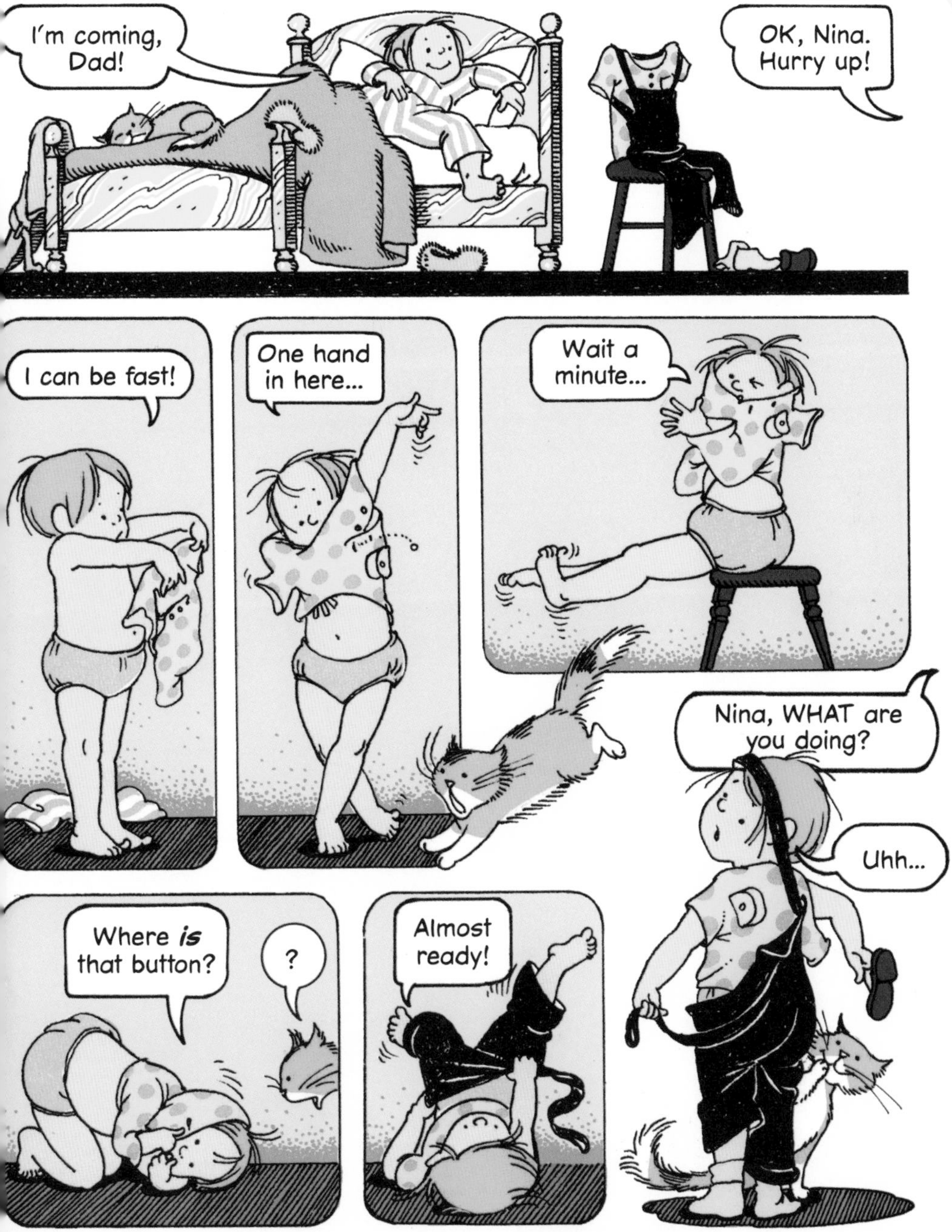
I'm coming, Dad!
OK, Nina. Hurry up!
I can be fast!
One hand in here...
Wait a minute...
Nina, WHAT are you doing?
Uhh...
Where *is* that button?
?
Almost ready!

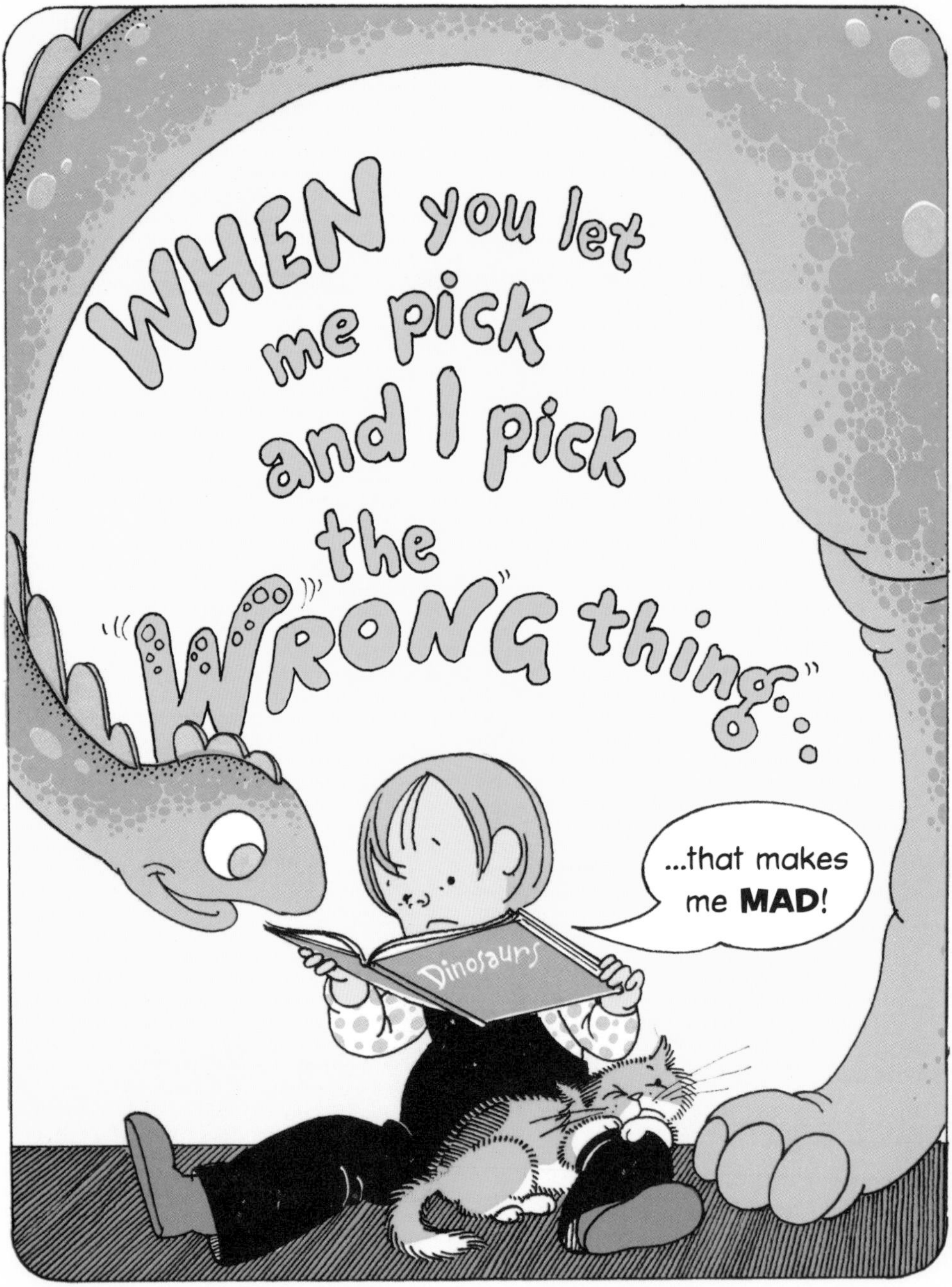
WHEN you let me pick and I pick the "WRONG" thing...
...that makes me **MAD**!
Dinosaurs

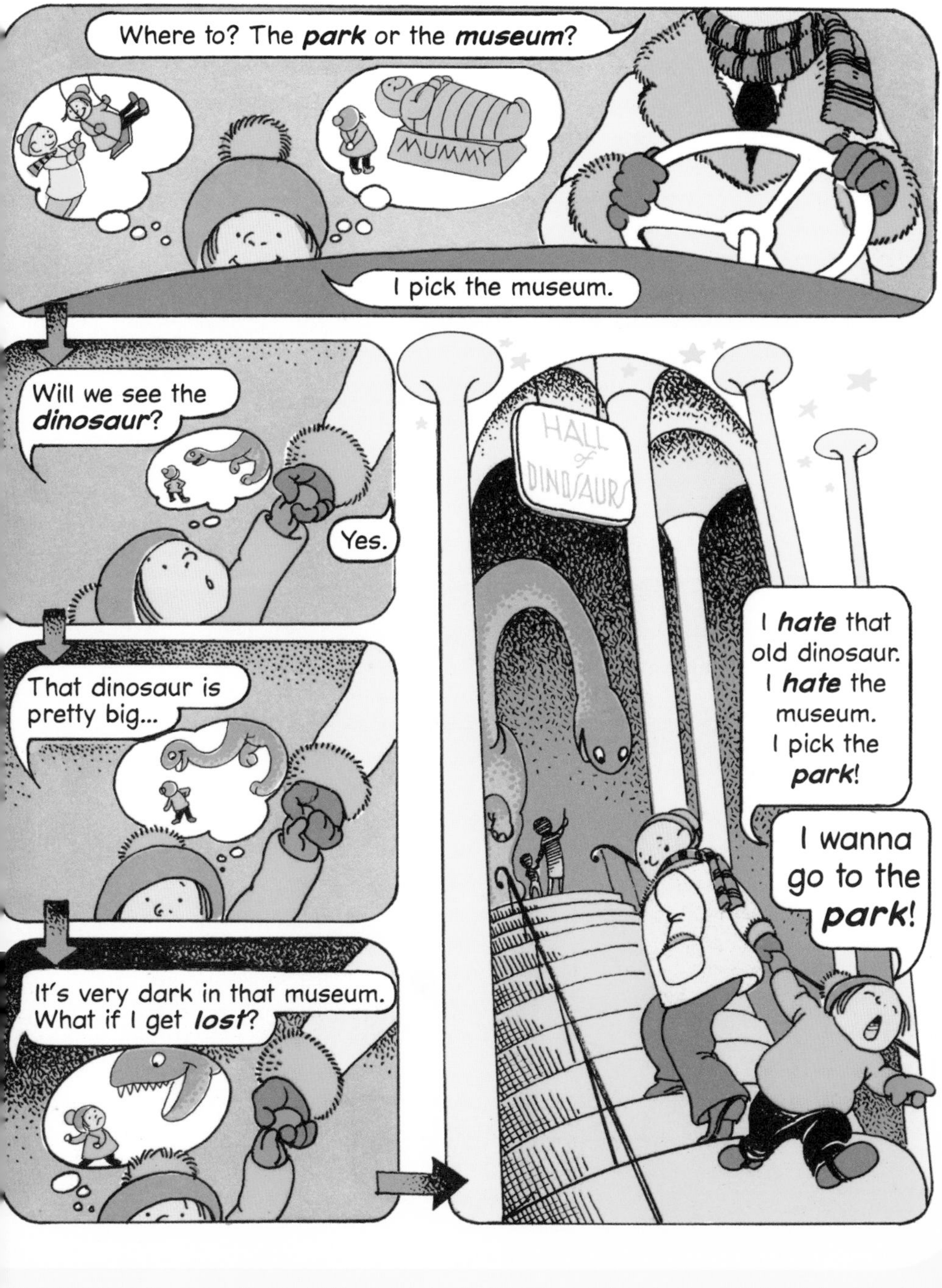
Where to? The *park* or the *museum*?
MUMMY
I pick the museum.
Will we see the *dinosaur*?
Yes.
That dinosaur is pretty big...
It's very dark in that museum. What if I get *lost*?
HALL of DINOSAURS
I *hate* that old dinosaur. I *hate* the museum. I pick the *park*!
I wanna go to the *park*!

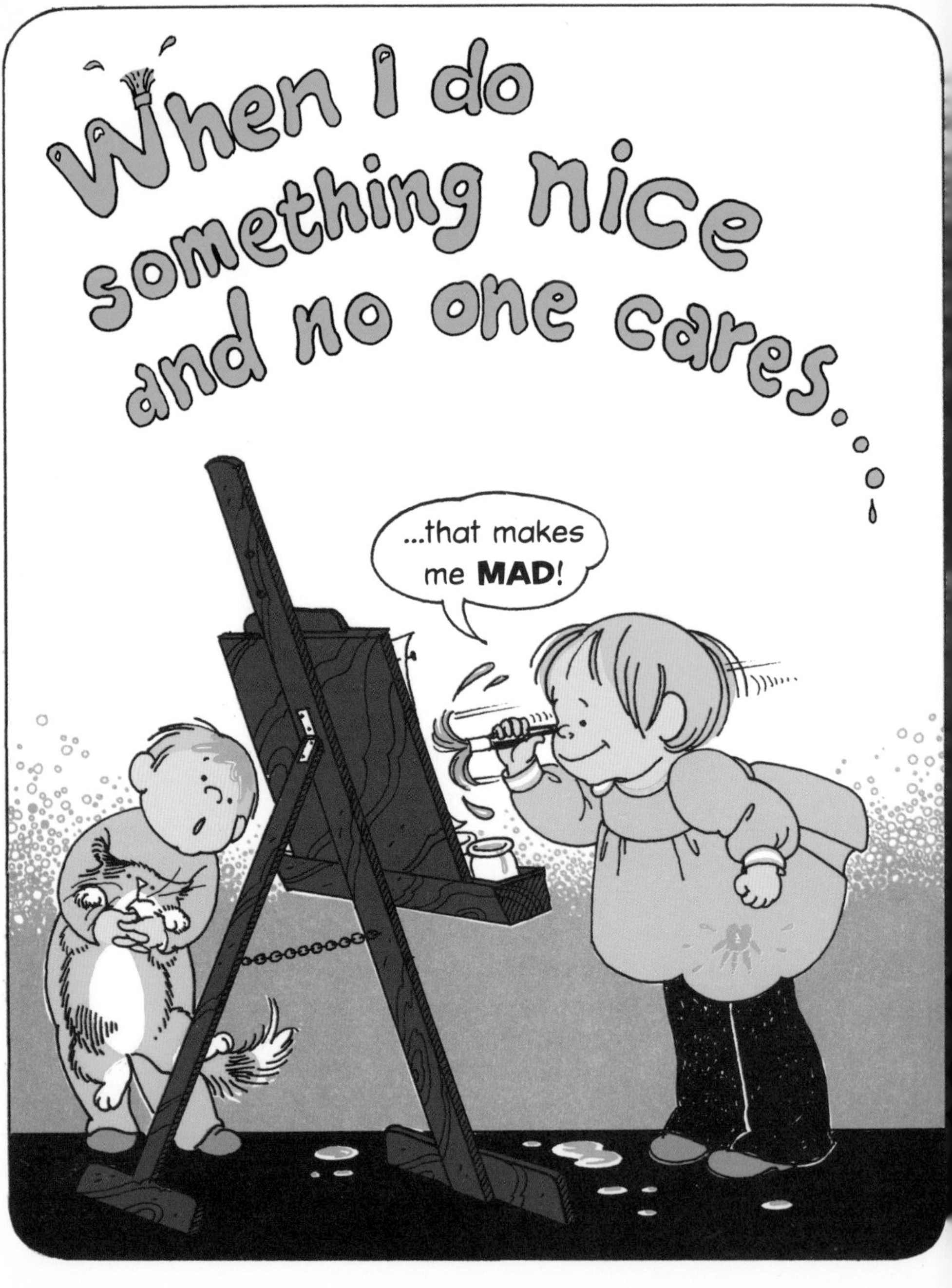
When I do something nice and no one cares...
...that makes me **MAD**!

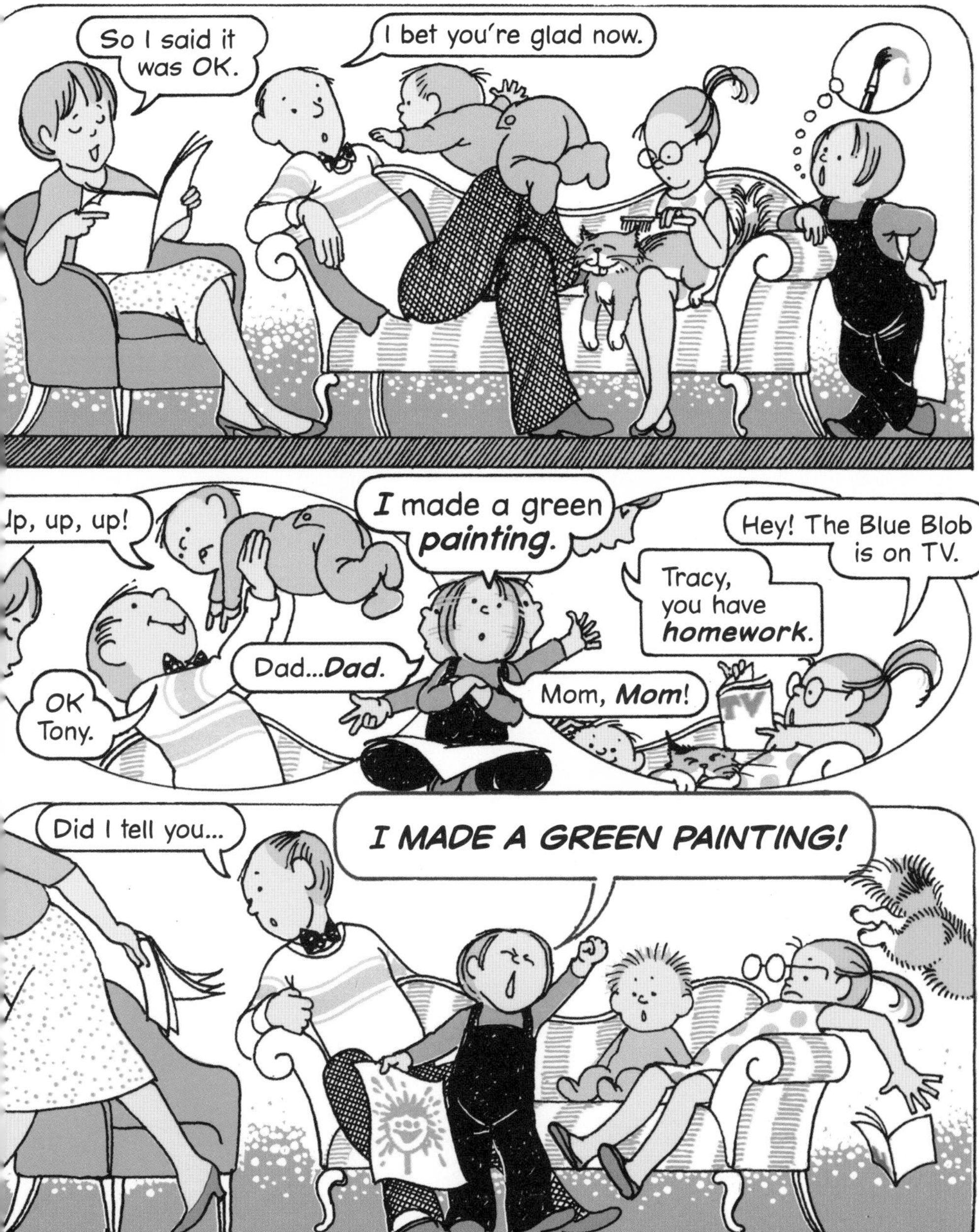

So I said it was OK.
I bet you're glad now.
Up, up, up!
OK Tony.
Dad...Dad.
I made a green painting.
Mom, Mom!
Tracy, you have homework.
Hey! The Blue Blob is on TV.
TV
Did I tell you...
I MADE A GREEN PAINTING!

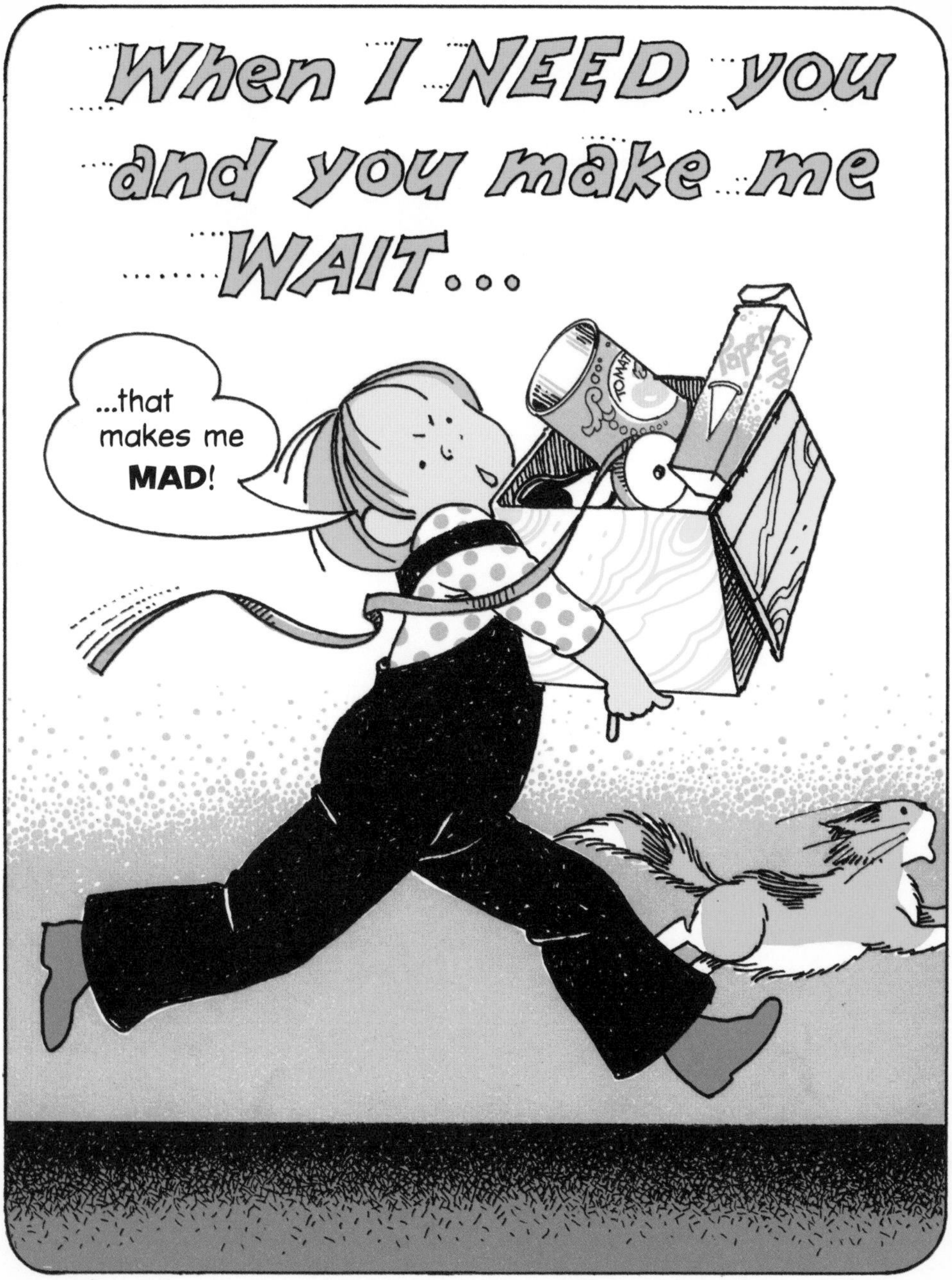
When I NEED you and you make me WAIT...
...that makes me **MAD**!
TOMATO
Paper Cups

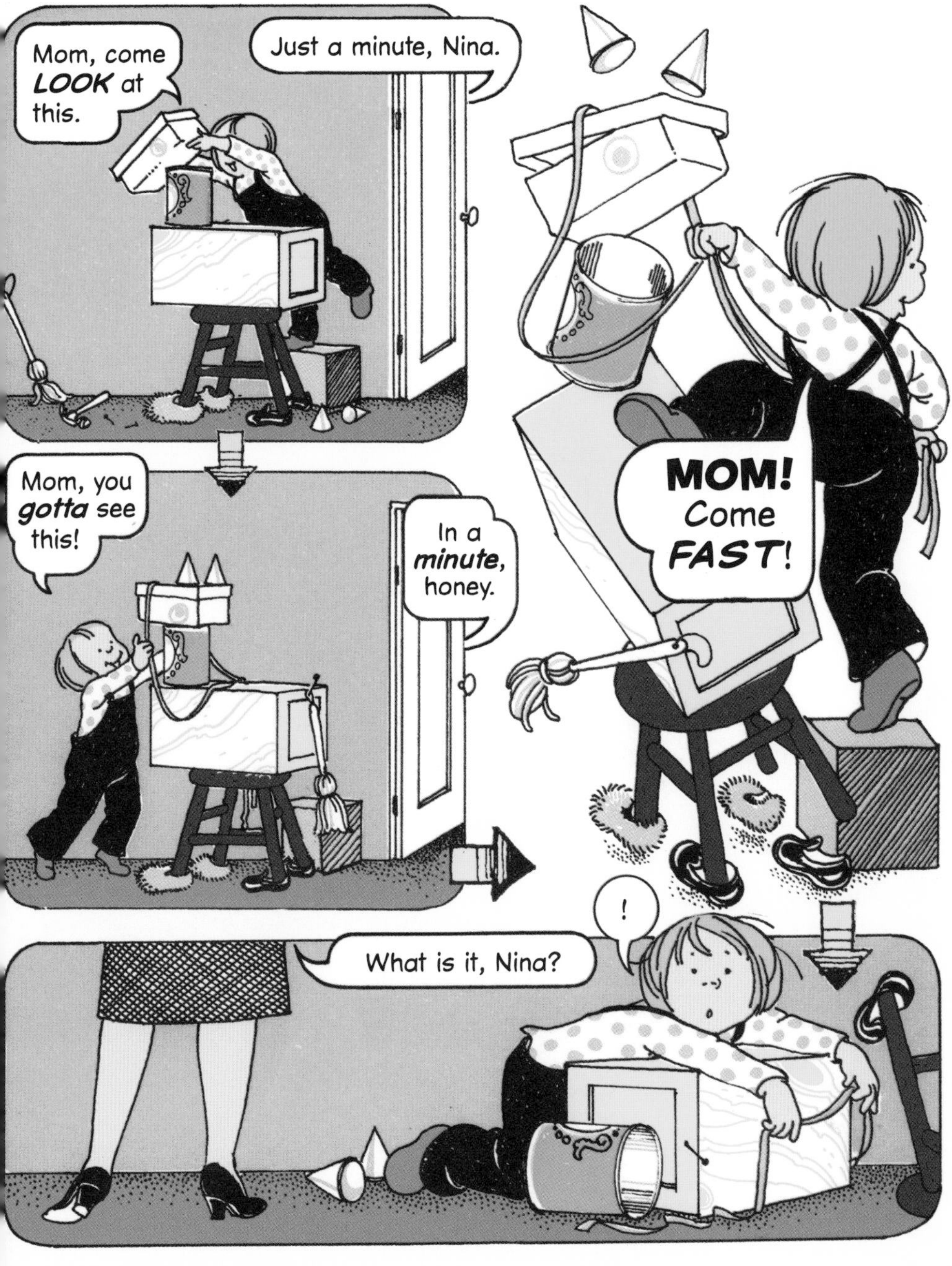

Mom, come **LOOK** at this.
Just a minute, Nina.
Mom, you *gotta* see this!
In a *minute*, honey.
MOM! Come *FAST*!
!
What is it, Nina?

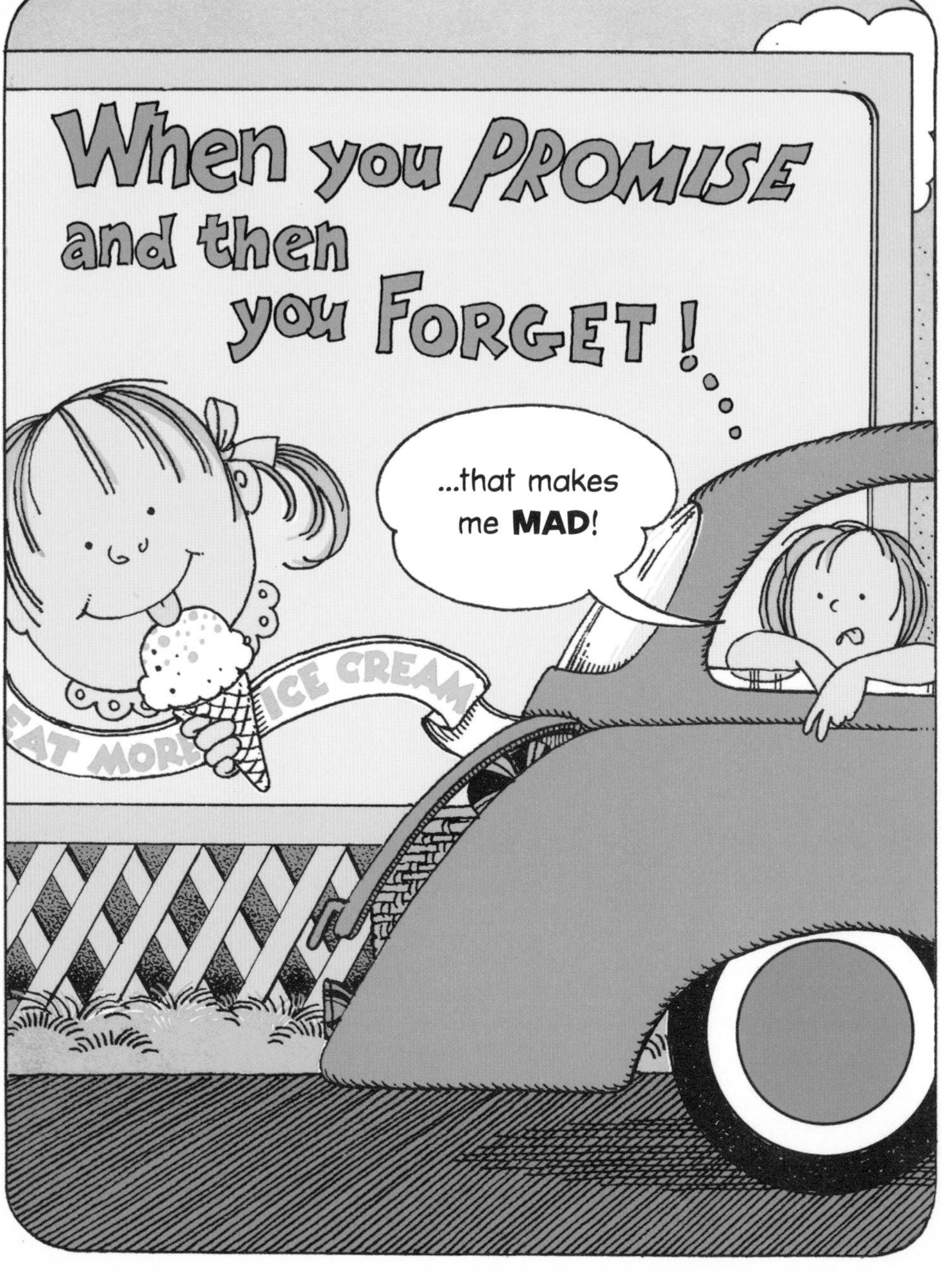
When you PROMISE
and then
you FORGET!
...that makes
me MAD!
EAT MORE ICE CREAM

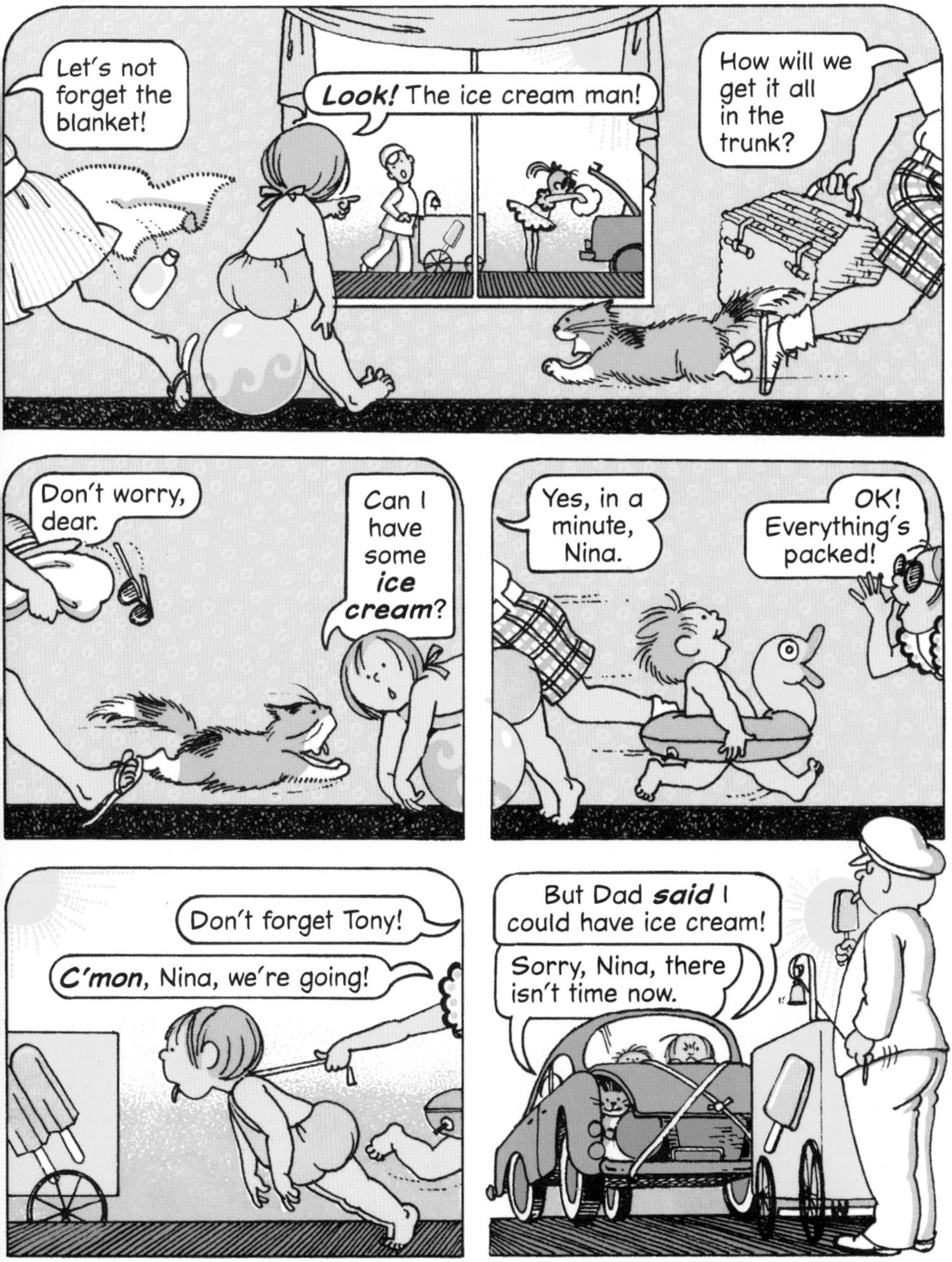
Let's not forget the blanket!
Look! The ice cream man!
How will we get it all in the trunk?
Don't worry, dear.
Can I have some ice cream?
Yes, in a minute, Nina.
OK! Everything's packed!
Don't forget Tony!
C'mon, Nina, we're going!
But Dad said I could have ice cream!
Sorry, Nina, there isn't time now.

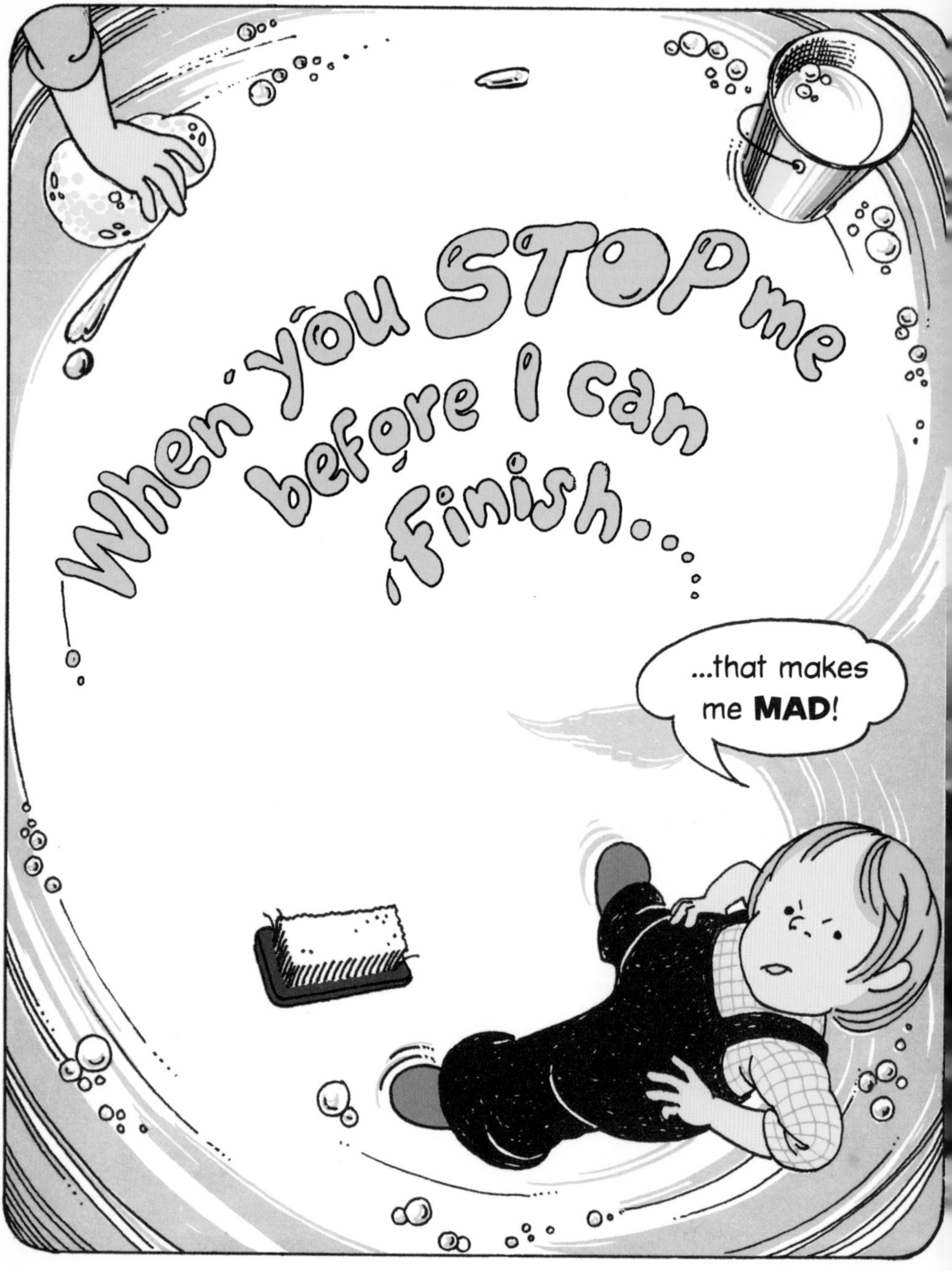
When you STOP me before I can finish...
...that makes me MAD!

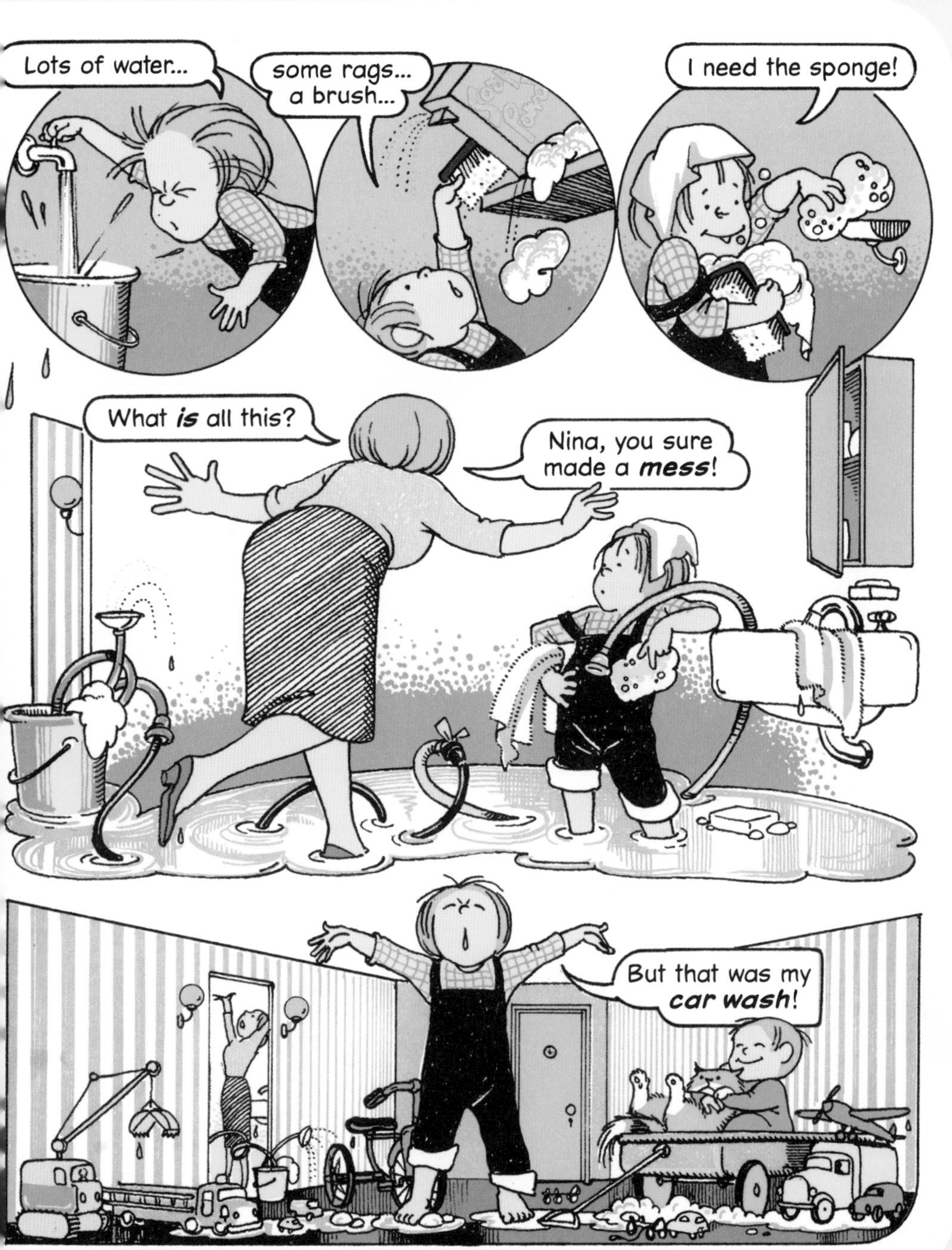
Lots of water...
some rags... a brush...
I need the sponge!
What *is* all this?
Nina, you sure made a ***mess***!
But that was my ***car wash***!

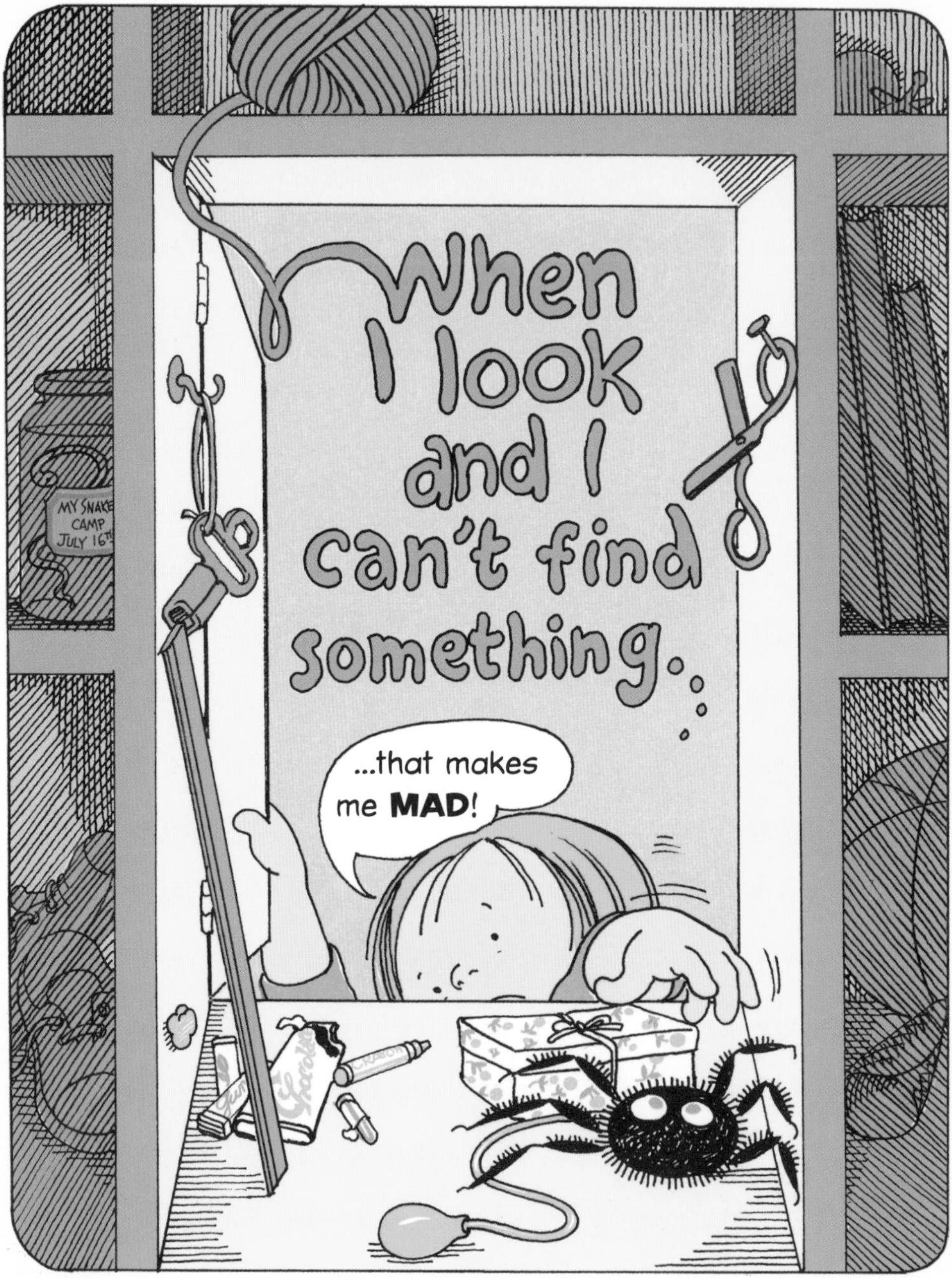
When I look and I can't find something...
...that makes me MAD!
MY SNAKE CAMP JULY 16TH

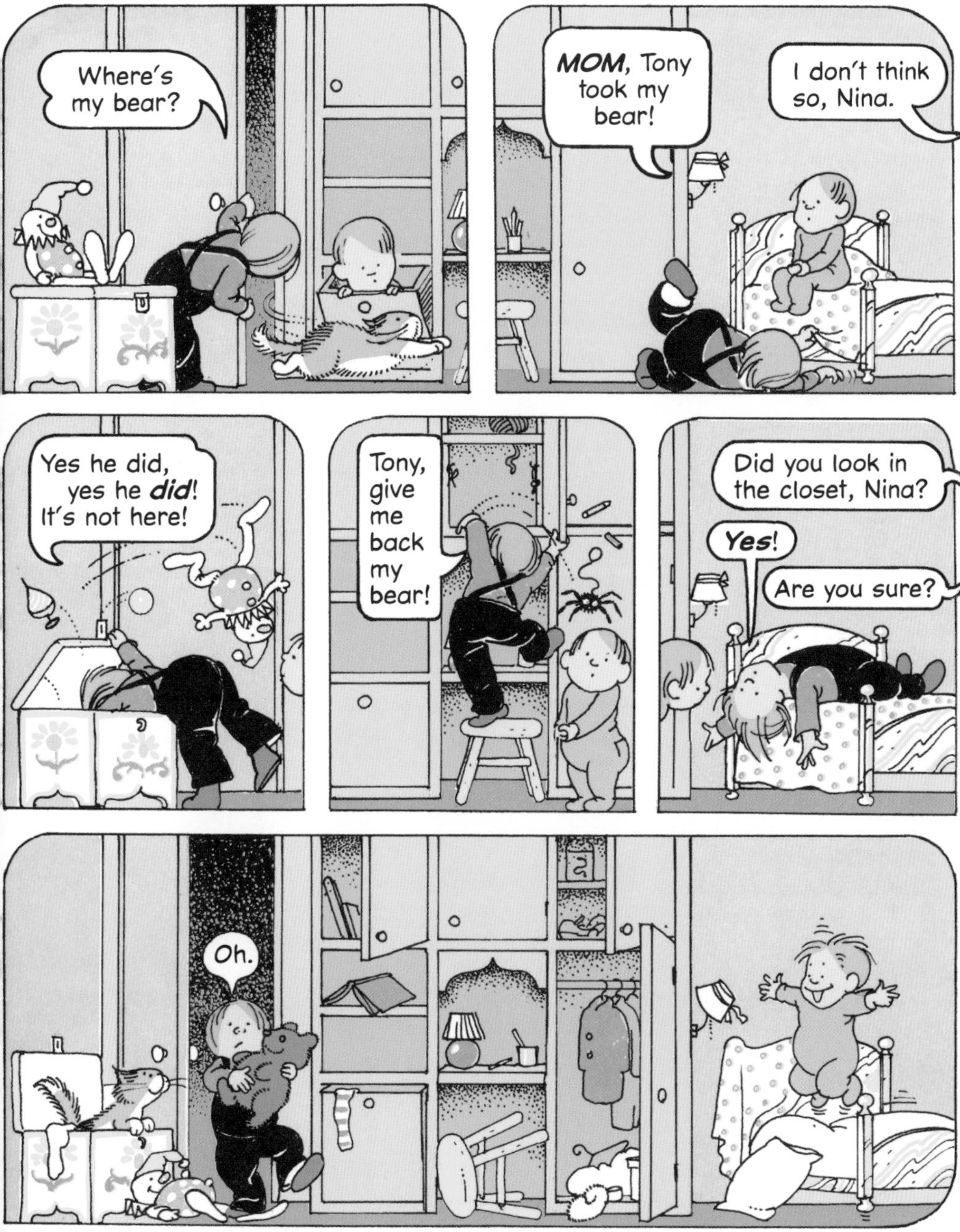
Where's my bear?
MOM, Tony took my bear!
I don't think so, Nina.
Yes he did, yes he did! It's not here!
Tony, give me back my bear!
Did you look in the closet, Nina?
Yes!
Are you sure?
Oh.

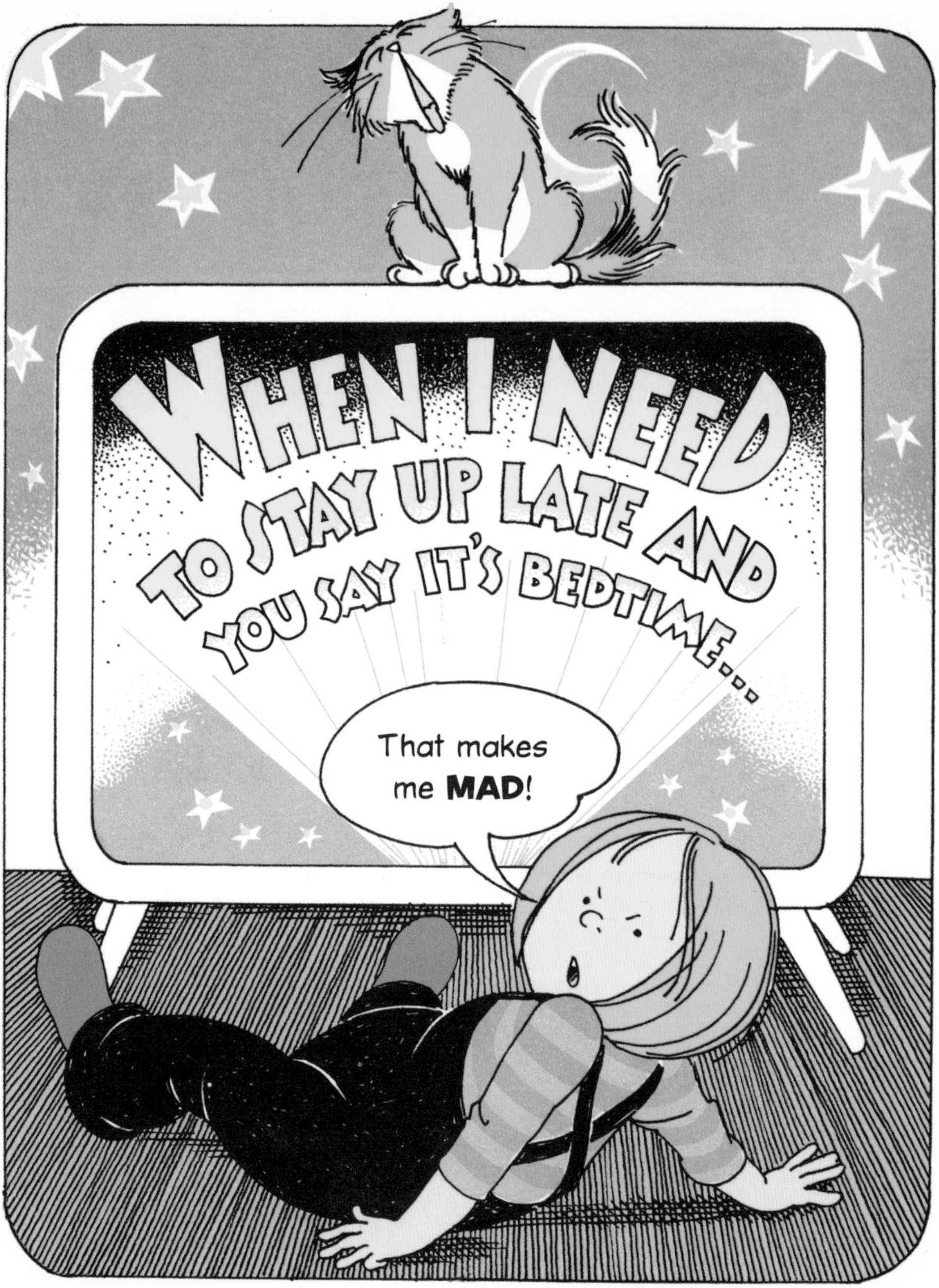
WHEN I NEED
TO STAY UP LATE AND
YOU SAY IT'S BEDTIME...
That makes me **MAD**!

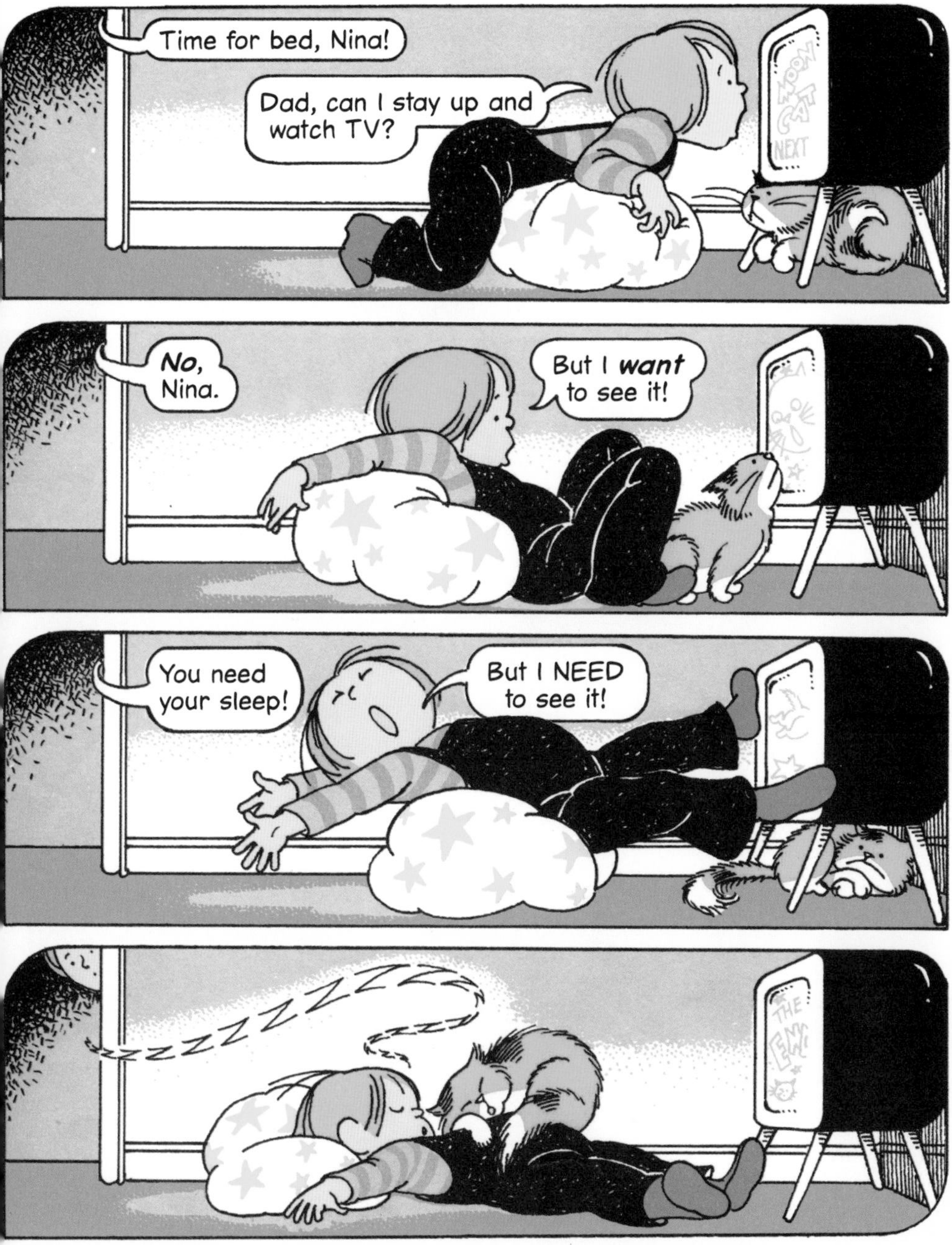

Time for bed, Nina!
Dad, can I stay up and watch TV?
MOON CAT NEXT
No, Nina.
But I want to see it!
You need your sleep!
But I NEED to see it!
ZZZZZZZZZZZZZZZZ
THE END

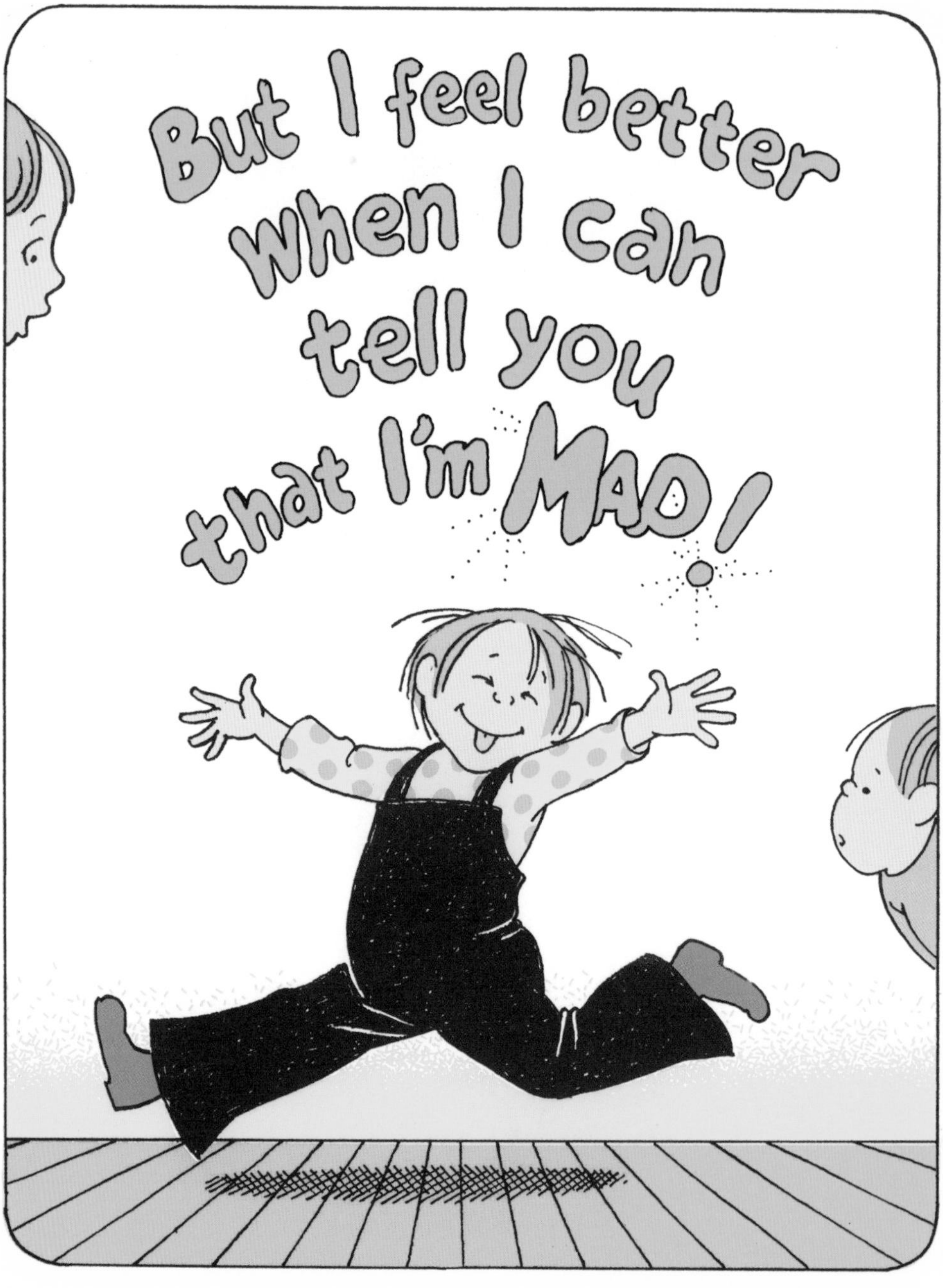
But I feel better
when I can
tell you
that I'm MAD!

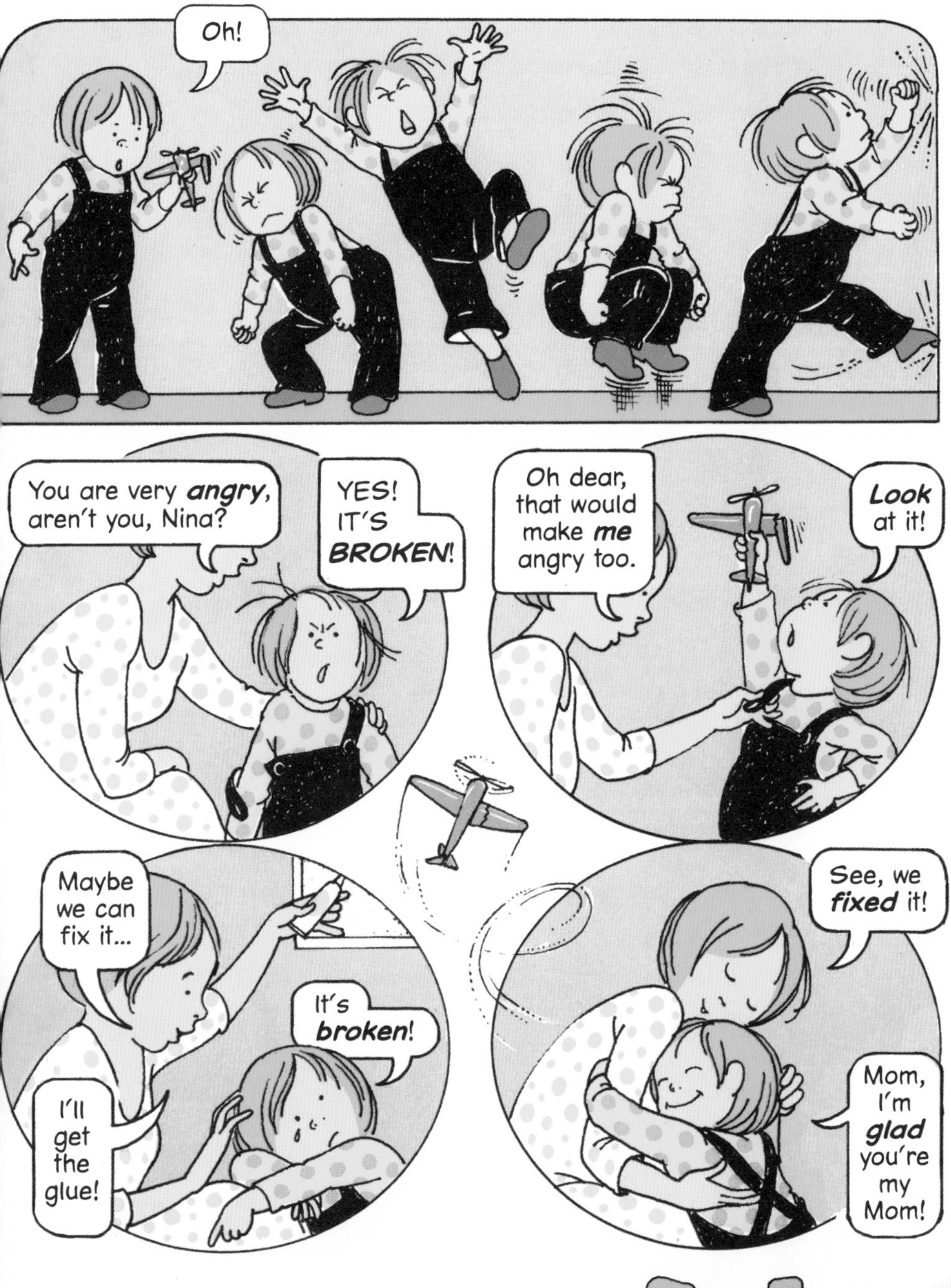
Oh!
You are very angry, aren't you, Nina?
YES! IT'S BROKEN!
Oh dear, that would make me angry too.
Look at it!
Maybe we can fix it...
It's broken!
I'll get the glue!
See, we fixed it!
Mom, I'm glad you're my Mom!
THE END

ABOUT THE AUTHORS

HILARY KNIGHT is the son of two accomplished artist-writers, Clayton Knight and Katherine Sturges, who collaborated on this classic *New Yorker* cover (Katherine penciled and Clayton inked it.)

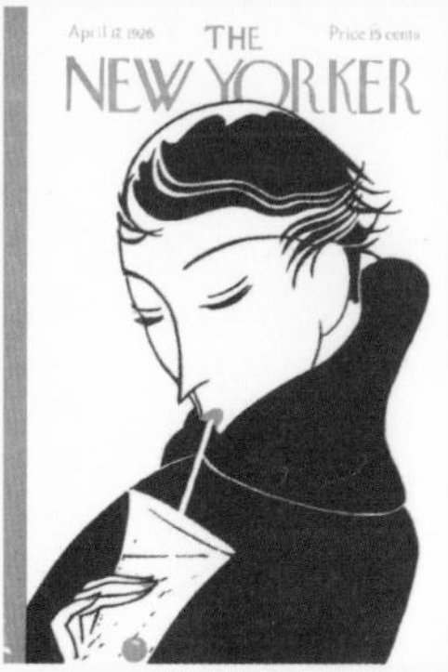
April 17, 1926
THE
NEW YORKER
Price 15 cents

Hilary Knight came into his own enormous success by illustrating Kay Thompson's *Eloise*, which has been a cultural touchstone for generations. He has written and illustrated nine children's books and illustrated over fifty more. He has also produced many magazine illustrations, record-album covers, and posters for Broadway musicals.

STEVEN KROLL wrote nearly a hundred books for children. He has said, "When I'm working on a book, I see the pictures as I write the words. How fortunate that the illustrators of my books have all seen what I've seen and have captured the magic I wish to share."

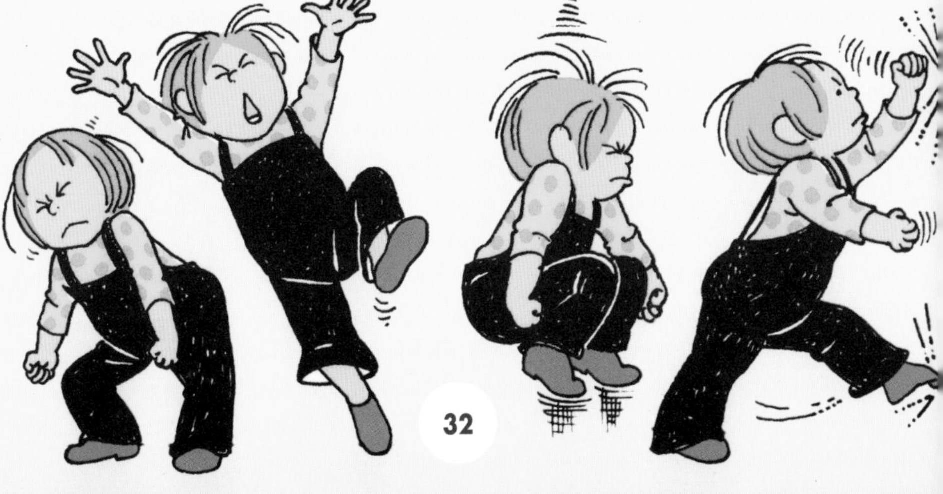

HOW TO "TOON INTO READING"
in a few simple steps:

Our goal is to get kids reading—and we know kids LOVE comics. We publish award-winning early readers in comics form for elementary and early middle school, and present them in three levels.

1 FIND THE RIGHT BOOK

Veteran teacher Cindy Rosado tells what makes a good book for beginning and struggling readers alike: "A vetted vocabulary, plenty of picture clues, repetition, and a clear and compelling story. Also, the book shouldn't be too easy—or the reader won't learn, but neither should it be too hard—or he or she may get discouraged."

The TOON INTO READING!™ program is designed for beginning readers and works wonders with reluctant readers.

MO AND JO
FIGHTING TOGETHER FOREVER
BENJAMIN BEAR
in Fuzzy Thinking
ZIG AND WIKKI
NADJA SPIEGELMAN & TRADE LOEFFLER
BENNY AND PENNY
THE BIG NO-NO!
Oh, Benny, this is a very big NO-NO!
Yes!
GEOFFREY HAYES
CHICK & CHICKIE
PLAY ALL DAY!
What do you want to play?
Claude Ponti
Little Mouse Gets Ready
THAT'S ME!
Jeff Smith
THE SHARK KING
JOHNSON

2 TAKE TIME WITH SILENT PANELS

Comics use panels to mark time, and silent panels count. Look and "read" even when there are no words. Often, humor is all in the timing!

KNOCK! KNOCK!
TRICK OR TREAT!

3 GUIDE YOUNG READERS

What works?

Keep your fingertip <u>below</u> the character that is speaking.

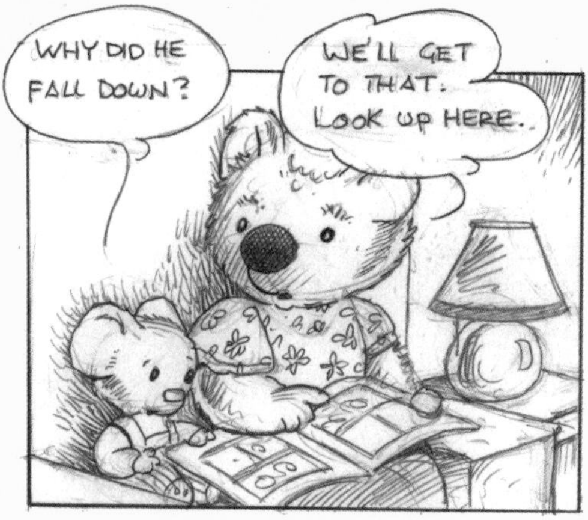
WHY DID HE FALL DOWN?
WE'LL GET TO THAT. LOOK UP HERE.

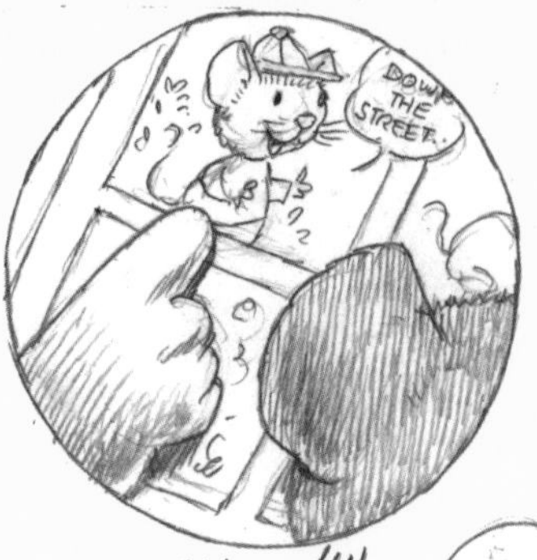
DOWN THE STREET.

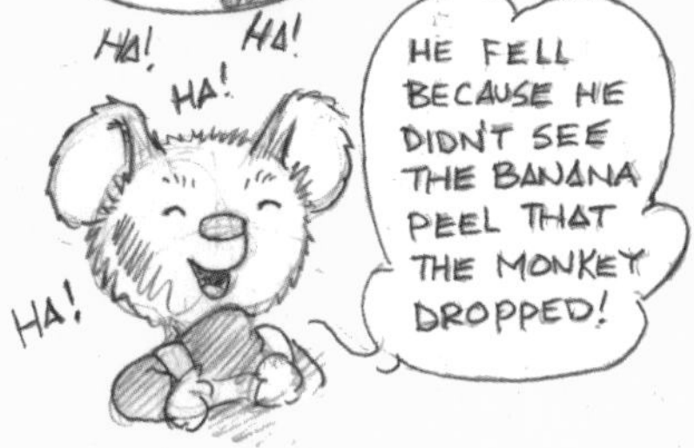
HA! HA! HA! HA!
HE FELL BECAUSE HE DIDN'T SEE THE BANANA PEEL THAT THE MONKEY DROPPED!

4 LET THE PICTURES TELL THE STORY

In a comic, you can often read the story even if you don't know all the words. Encourage young readers to tell you what's happening based on the facial expressions and body language.

5 GET OUT THE CRAYONS

Kids see the hand of the author in a comic and it makes them want to tell their own stories. Encourage them to talk, write and draw!

Get kids talking, and you'll be surprised at how perceptive they are about pictures.

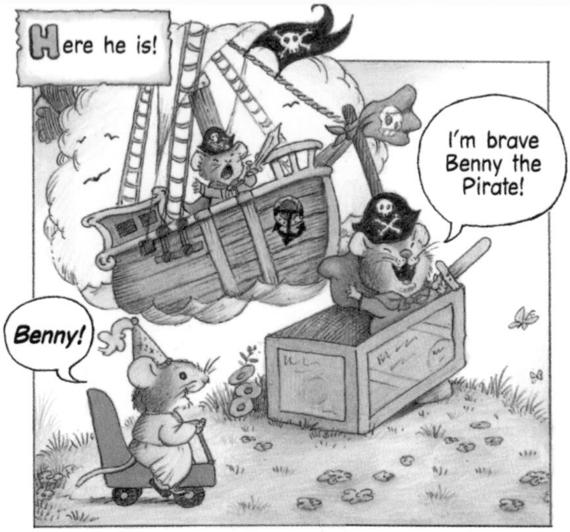
Here he is!
I'm brave Benny the Pirate!
Benny!

6 LET THEM GUESS

Comics provide a large amount of context for the words, so let young readers make informed guesses, and don't over-correct. In this panel, the artist shows a pirate ship, two pirate hats, and two pirate flags the first time the word "PIRATE" is introduced.